Ucko, Peter 73
Ulpunyaii ochre source 111, 195
Uluru (Ayers Rock) 85, 101, 289, 290
'Undiara' 103
Unggumi 105
Ungud (the Rainbow Serpent) 112
'Uniformitarianism' 89
United States 185, 278
univariate analyses 203
Unmatjera 102
unpatinated 99, 245
Upside Down Man Shelter 181
uranium series 10

Valcamonica 150, 151, 158, 277
vandalism 85, 248, 281, 282, 283
Venus figurines 183
Veth, Peter 13, 14
Vezere (France) 277
Victoria 12, 18, 24, 37, 142, 286
Victoria River District 36, 47–9, 57, 60,
    82, 86, 128, 165
Vinnicombe, Patricia ix, 70, 75, 156, 175,
    176, 177, 198, 281
visitors 85, 280–90 passim
Vogelherd 65
von Sturmer, John 114
vulva 210, 215, 216, 217, 218, 225

Wadgalang 206
waisted blades 10, 17
Walaemini 262
Walbiri 95, 96, 97, 100, 102
Walinga Hill Cave 42, 103, 116
Walker, Frederick 233
Walk-Under-Arch Shelter 19, 132, 141
Wallace Rockhole 307
Wallace's Line 6
Walsh, Grahame 52, 53, 77, 125, 144, 284,
    290, 294

Walsh–Mitchell Rivers 63
Wanang Ngari Aboriginal Corporation 301,
    303, 304
Wanderers' Cave 208
Wandjina 48, 52, 53, 60, 84, 105, 106,
    107, 112, 116, 125, 135, 144, 146,
    163, 164, 168, 189, 196, 301–5
Wandjuk Marika 300
'waninga' (stringed crosses) 101
Ward, Graeme 81, 82
Ward River 205
Wardaman 48
Wargata Mina Cave (Judd's Cavern) 43,
    136
Warramunga 102
Warreen 42
Warrego River 205, 207, 216, 227
Watchman, Alan 78, 82, 132, 138, 140,
    267, 268, 297, 298
watercraft 6, 9, 18, 55
Waterfall Cave 138, 139
waterholes 101, 160, 187
Wave Hill Station 83
weapons 16, 19, 39, 101, 146, 148, 159,
    162, 163, 166, 175, 176
the Weir 295
Welch, David 52, 162
Wellman, K. ix, 68
Western Australia 18, 19, 78, 84, 110, 111,
    120, 121, 129, 136, 137, 142, 190,
    280, 285, 292, 296, 298, 303
Western Desert 39, 92, 100, 102, 116,
    184, 185, 301
Whale Cave 280
White Mountains 246
Wiessner, Polly 117
Wilga Mia ochre quarry 110–11, 195
Willcox, Bert 69

Winnininnie 40, 98
Winterbotham 28
WL3 burial site (at Lake Mungo) 140
Wobst, Martin 75, 117
Wodai estates 106
Wollongong 280
Woodside petroleum-drilling 280
Woorabinda 233
World Heritage Committee and World
    Heritage Fund 277
World Heritage Convention (of UNESCO)
    267, 277
Worora 105, 106
Worsnop, Thomas 211
Wright, Bruce 54
Wright, Richard 260, 263
Wunambel 105
wunan 106, 107, 189
Wyrie Swamp 17

X–ray
    diffraction spectrometry (XRD) 79, 196
    fluorescence spectroscopy (XRF) 79
    style xi, 15, 47, 49, 50, 93, 139, 160,
        171, 173

yam 19, 21, 141, 171, 257, 264
Yam Camp 46, 270
Yam Painting Style 161, 194
Yangaru and Wuturu moieties 207, 208
Yarrowich art site 289
Yingalarri (Ingalaadi) 48, 49, 57, 128
Yirritja 108, 109
Yirrkalla 97, 110, 112
Yolngu 107–10
Yumbulul, Terry 300
Yuwunggayai Shelter 52, 126

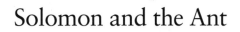

Solomon and the Ant

By Sheldon Oberman

The Always Prayer Shawl
By the Hanukkah Light
The Folk Festival Book
Island of the Minotaur: Greek Myths of Ancient Crete
Julie Gerond and the Polka Dot Pony
The Lion in the Lake
Mirror of a People
The Shaman's Nephew: A Life in the Far North
This Business with Elijah
TV Sal and the Game Show from Outer Space
The White Stone in the Castle Wall
The Wisdom Bird: A Tale of Solomon and Sheba

SOLOMON AND THE ANT

AND OTHER JEWISH FOLKTALES

RETOLD BY
Sheldon Oberman

INTRODUCTION AND COMMENTARY BY
Peninnah Schram

Boyds Mills Press
Honesdale, Pennsylvania

To my children, Adam, Mira, and Jesse—
may the legacy of storytelling continue
—S.O.

Text copyright © 2006 by the Estate of Sheldon Oberman
Introduction, commentary, and expanded sources and variants
copyright © 2006 by Peninnah Schram

Boyds Mills Press, Inc.
815 Church Street
Honesdale, Pennsylvania 18431
Printed in China

LIBRARY OF CONGRESS CATALOGING-IN-PUBLICATION DATA
Oberman, Sheldon.
Solomon and the ant: and other Jewish folktales / retold by Sheldon Oberman;
Summary: A chronologically arranged collection of more than forty
Jewish folktales with commentary, including
"The Seven Questions of Alexander the Great,"
"A Special Way of Thinking," and "Which One Was Blind?"
Includes bibliographical references.
ISBN-13: 978-1-59078-307-8
ISBN-10: 1-59078-307-7 (alk. paper)
1. Jews—Folklore. 2. Tales. [1. Jews—Folklore. 2. Folklore.]
I. Schram, Peninnah. II. Title.
PZ8.1.O225Sol 2006
398.2'089'924—dc22   2005020115

First edition
10 9 8 7 6 5 4 3

Contents

Introduction 7

Solomon and the Ant 17

The Smell of Money 19

The Starling's Answer 23

Solomon's Ring of Wisdom 27

Enough 32

Golden Plates 38

The Seven Questions of
    Alexander the Great 42

Who Knows? 45

The Special Ingredient 48

A Special Way of Thinking 51

The Magic Seed 55

The True Jewel of Their Father 58

The Worst Poison 61

The Inquisitor's Test 65

The Wisdom of a Bird 67

The Wound That Did Not Heal 70

The Mouse That Went
    Looking for a Husband 75

Teaching a Wolf 79

What Do You Want to Be? 81

Sharp as a Diamond 86

Give Her What You Want 89

The Rich Man's Reward 93

The Shepherd's Pipe 96

Don't Ask 100

Changing a Mind 104

Softening a Heart 106

The Coachman's Answer 107

The Prince Who Thought
    He Was a Rooster 111

Things Should Match 115

Juha's Nail 121

What His Father Did 126

Tales of Chelm 127

    The Wrong Kind of Horse 127

    How Not to Train a Cow 127

    A Lot of Sense 128

    Chelm Law 129

A Holy Fool 131

Which One Was More Blind? 133

A Head Full of Dreams 134

The Riddling Woman 137

The Hiding Place 144

The Crowded House 147

Never Afraid Again 150

The Best Merchandise 153

Epilogue 155

Glossary 156

Bibliography 161

Introduction
by Peninnah Schram

THIS COLLECTION OF JEWISH FOLKTALES REVEALS MANY FACETS OF the Jewish people. Throughout Jewish history, Jews developed an oral expertise in their learning of Torah and Talmud. In addition, Jews honed necessary verbal skills in their business dealings and relationships in countries with Arabic or Christian rulers as well as their non-Jewish neighbors. These skills included all types of mental and verbal abilities, such as clever and resourceful reasoning, debating, quick wit, plays on words, and tricky responses in tight situations. In turn, this virtuoso verbal mastery has determined the types of folktales that have been passed down through the generations. But the wit has always been applied with wisdom, never for deception or cleverness for its own sake. When the stories strike a chord within us—often because of surprise endings, the use of metaphors, vivid language, exaggeration, fantastic characters, heroes and heroines, challenging problems, and other rhetorical devices—they offer us this wisdom (or *khokhma*) and remain with us for easy retrieval when needed. In that way, when Jews have needed that wisdom, the tales have been there in our "well of wisdom" to draw from.

These humorous stories do not always create a laughing response on the part of the reader or listener. They are not always "ha-ha" funny. Instead of a burst of out-loud laughter, the response may be more of an inner "aha" or "ah" or just a smile of recognition or a nod of the head. These kinds of stories offer us a sense of perspective. They might even lift a cloud from our hearts. They restore hope and faith in God. They put us on the right path. Teaching, always teaching.

And that is what the reteller, Sheldon Oberman, had intended. In addition to the stories, brief Jewish historical notes are interwoven throughout the book to help put the stories into a context.

The sequence of the stories is arranged chronologically through history, as much as possible. Some stories take place during a specific historical time, while others might have been told during that time period. However, all of the stories are part of the Jewish repertoire. The book begins with the biblical characters Solomon and Elijah, who become transformed in folktales into two of the most important and popular folklore heroes in Jewish oral tradition. Then there are stories associated with the Talmudic period, including some with non-Jewish heroes who actually appear in Jewish folklore, such as Emperor Antoninus and Alexander the Great. The next series of stories takes place after the Roman period and into the medieval centuries. And finally, there are many folktales that bring us to more contemporary times, when Jews traveled to different countries throughout the world.

In this collection there are examples of many genres of stories, such as legends of King Solomon (the first four tales), religious tales (Elijah tales: "Enough!" and "Golden Plates"; "Who Knows?" with Rabbi Akiva; and "Shepherd's Pipe" with the Baal Shem Tov), medieval fables (such as "The Wisdom of a Bird," "The Wound That Did Not Heal," "The Mouse that Went Looking for a Husband," and "Teaching a Wolf"), wisdom tales ("The Best Merchandise" and "Never Afraid Again"), anecdotal tales ("Sharp as a Diamond" and "The Crowded House"), trickster tales ("Juha's Nail" and "What His Father Did"), Chelm "fool" stories ("A Lot of Sense" and "Wrong Kind of a Horse"), holy fool tale ("A Holy Fool"), riddle stories ("The Seven Questions of Alexander the Great" and "The Riddling Woman"), and more.

While many of these stories are associated only with a specific person or period within Jewish folklore, one can also find versions of the same story told with a different hero. Such is the case with "The Coachman's Answer," which is most often told with the Dubner Maggid and his coachman. But there are versions found elsewhere with a different rabbi. Or else the time period gets changed into more modern times, as in these versions of "The Crowded House" and "Never Afraid Again."

As is the case with many Jewish folktales, variants are also found in world folklore. Because of the fluid folklore process, many tales in the Jewish oral tradition resemble tales in universal folklore. While many of the tales originated in Jewish sources (Torah, Talmud, Rabbinic tales, and so on), many became adapted into the folktales of other cultures and other religions. The obverse is also true. Many folktales that stem from other cultures and religions were transformed into Jewish stories, as long as the themes, values, and ethical lessons in those stories also resonated in Judaism. (In other words, just changing the names of the characters to Jewish names will not create a Jewish version of any story without the main criteria noted above.)

Since Jews have lived in most parts of the world, there has always been a strong influence of the dominant culture on the Jews. In many ways, Jews are chameleon-like in that there is a great deal of assimilation, or melding, of foods, names, clothing, folkways, and folklore from the particular culture in which they are living. However, the normative Jewish religion has always remained true to its core beliefs. Thus, there were strong cross-cultural contacts; for example, with the Arabic culture in Spain and throughout the Middle Eastern countries, especially in the realm of folkways, folktales, and folksongs.

In the telling and retelling of the adapted stories, the tales began to mirror the cultural and religious contexts of the storytellers and soon became the carriers of Jewish values and traditions. For example, in earlier Jewish fables, many of which were translated and adapted from Indian, Roman, and Greek sources, the animals were not only endowed with human personalities but also spoke wisely about Torah, quoting biblical and Talmudic passages.

As a further example, there are several stories in this collection that embody a similar theme that especially resonates in Judaism, that a person should be happy or satisfied with who he is and with what he has. ("The Mouse That Went Looking for a Husband," "The Coachman's Answer," "The Crowded House," and "What Do You Want to Be?"). There is always a compelling reason why a certain story continues to be told in a culture over the generations: primarily because of the importance or emphasis of its teaching. This theme reminds me of the extraordinary Chasidic story of Reb Zusya of Hanipol who said, "In Paradise, they won't ask me: 'Why weren't you like Moses?' but rather, 'Why weren't you like Zusya?'" The theme is echoed in "The Ethics of the Fathers," too, when the question is asked, "Who is rich?" The answer given is "The man who is content with what he has."

So our stories come from near and far, some from Jewish sources and many transformed from other cultures. Isaac Disraeli understood this when he wrote: "Tales have wings, whether they come from the East or from the North, and they soon become denizens wherever they alight."

This can be seen in the examination of tales collected in the Israel Folktale Archives (IFA). Founded by folklorist Dov Noy in 1955, the IFA has collected more than twenty-three thousand folktales from the various ethnic communities who now live in Israel. The stories have been classified according to tale type and motifs. Throughout this book, there are notations of the tales that have variants found in the Israel Folktale Archives. This clearly shows how tales circulate and become adapted to different cultures, within the Jewish oral tradition and in that of other countries.

From antiquity into the present, the Jewish people have had a dynamic interaction between text and the oral tradition. From the beginning, Jews have had a great respect for orality. Being the oral storyteller he was, Sheldon Oberman retained an orality in his versions of these folktales. He employed dialogue and simple sentences, vernacular language, and so on. These stories, when read aloud, sound as though he was telling them directly to the reader. Actually, even when one thinks of reading as "silent," research has found that there is always an interaction that takes place between the reader and the print that, in turn, makes the words spring off the page. That is an art achieved by Sheldon Oberman!

Solomon and the Ant and Other Jewish Folktales is a book that I expected to read only after its publication; I did not expect to participate in editing it. However, when the author-storyteller Sheldon Oberman (or Obie, as he was called by his friends) suffered from a serious illness early in 2004, he asked me if I would complete this book for him. I agreed with my whole heart, as I regarded this task as a sacred responsibility. At the time, I still hoped he would heal and recover enough strength to finish the book himself, or at least that he would be able to confer with me during the final drafts. That was not to be. Sheldon Oberman died on March 26, 2004. I only hope and pray that I have fulfilled Obie's expectations. Sheldon Oberman did not live to actually hold this book in his hands; nevertheless, he held the stories in his heart.

In his first anthology of Jewish folktales, Obie had left these forty-three stories, brief introductions to each story, after-story notes, and some sources for the stories. I have wanted to preserve as much of his voice and thoughts as possible. Therefore, I edited his words carefully and judiciously. My contribution to this book is in dialoguing with the stories and his notes through my commentary after his own notes to each story. In addition, I expanded the sources and variants list and also added tale types and motifs for most of the stories. I felt that this format would serve everyone better than if I were to merge my notes with his.

This book now serves as his legacy for all of us who will read and retell these stories. Just as Glueckl of Hamelyn wrote her diaries as an ethical will, so, too, is this book, along with all of Sheldon's other books of stories, his Ethical Will. He included stories that teach us traditions, values and lessons of Judaism. When stories come alive in the minds of the readers-listeners, the past is projected into the present, and, in turn, transmit cultural identity and self-knowledge.

One of the stories in this book, about the holy fool Reb Shmelke of Nikolsburg, reminded me of Obie. In the story, Reb Shmelke gives an old ring to a beggar asking for handouts. When Reb Shmelke's wife discovers this, she scolds him, telling him it was actually a valuable ring with a diamond. What does Reb Shmelke do? He doesn't try to get the ring back from the beggar.

Rather, he finds the beggar to advise him to get a good price for this ring. What's the connection that I made between the story and Obie? Apparently, in his spare time, Obie collected what he called "found objects" to create collage art. Once, he donated some items from his bric-a-brac collection to a friend holding a garage sale, and then went to the sale and bought them all back. As a "trickster" himself, he understood the beautiful value of *tzedakah*. (There are several stories that deal with this theme: "Don't Ask," "Changing a Mind," and "Softening a Heart.")

Obie has done something valuable with stories all his life. He collected and reworked the folktales. He "gave" them away through his tellings and writings. In this way, he gave them new life and helped to bring more justice and righteousness into our lives. His goal was always for us to go out to retell the stories so that Judaism would continue to thrive and remain vibrantly meaningful.

We are all fortunate that Sheldon Oberman was able to complete choosing the stories, retelling them in his voice, and adding notations that place the stories in a context for us. His legacy continues to live in this book.

Jewish Folktales

Solomon and the Ant

The Jewish people have a special love for tales of wisdom, cleverness, and tricks. You can find these tales as far back as the Bible. The snake "tricks" Eve into eating the apple, Abraham cleverly convinces God not to destroy Sodom and Gomorrah if he can find ten good people, and Isaac wisely asks an angel for a blessing after wrestling with the angel all through the night.

There are countless stories of wisdom, cleverness, and trickery told beyond the Biblical stories. There are *midrashim* created by the rabbis and folktales recounted by the common people about Biblical characters like Solomon, who lived three thousand years ago and was famous for his wisdom.

Many tales set out to prove that Solomon was the greatest and the wisest of all kings. It is natural for people to brag that their king is the very best.

People want to be proud of their leaders, but they don't want their leaders to be too proud of themselves. That's why some folktales set out to prove that no king, or any human being, is all powerful or all knowing.

The wonderful thing about King Solomon was that he was never too proud to learn. He was willing to learn from even the lowliest creature. In this tale, the great King Solomon is brought down to earth, but because he accepts the wisdom of a little ant, he becomes even greater than he was before.

SOLOMON HAD A MAGIC CARPET THAT ONLY HE COULD COMMAND. One day he was flying high above the earth, and he was very pleased with himself. He said, "I am the greatest of all. I fly above the world. I understand all the languages of all the creatures. I can even hear them speak from this great height."

At that moment he heard a creature say, "King Solomon is not so great."

Solomon looked down and saw that the words had been spoken by an ant. He commanded the carpet to stop and to descend to the earth. Solomon found the tiny ant. He bent down and picked it up so he could look at it eye to eye. He said to it, "You little creature of the dust, I heard you say that I am not so great. Tell me, who is greater than I am?"

The ant replied, "I am greater than you."

"How can you say that?" asked Solomon.

The ant answered, "I am greater than you."

"What!" said Solomon. "How?"

The ant replied, "I am greater than you because the greatest king in the world stopped when he heard me speak, he lowered himself to the earth, and he bent down in front of me. He raised me up so we were the same height, and he asked me a question that I could answer and he could not."

Solomon smiled. He said, "I am the king who stopped when you spoke and lowered himself, and bent down, raised you up, and asked you a question that he could not answer."

"You are," said the ant. "And I am the creature who told you something you did not know."

King Solomon gently lowered the ant back to the earth. "O wise and mighty Ant, you are greater than I thought you were, and I am not as great as I thought I was. I still have much to learn from my fellow creatures."

NOTE
In another folktale, Solomon halts his horse to avoid trampling some ants. He tells his companion, the Queen of Sheba, that to God, ants are just as important as people. In fact, when God looks down from the great height of Heaven, ants and humans look almost the same size.

COMMENTARY
The Talmud teaches us that humans can learn from everything, even from tiny ants. "Who teaches us by the beasts of the earth, and makes us wise by the fowls of heaven" (Job 35:11). Rabbi Yohanan said: "Had Torah not been given [to us], we could have learned modesty from the cat, avoiding seizure of others' property from the ant, avoidance of infidelity from the dove, and good manners from the rooster. . . ." (Eruvin 100b). This story can be connected with what Solomon wrote in Proverbs 6:6, "Go to the ant, consider her ways, and be wise."

SOURCES AND VARIANTS
"Solomon and the Ant" is part of a longer story in which Solomon is taught a humbling lesson about the dangers of arrogance and the misuse of his great wisdom and power.

The earlier versions of the full story can be found in *Ma'asseh ha-Namalah, Ma'asseh Nissim*, as well as in Louis Ginzberg's *The Legends of the Jews*, VI, with versions in Moses Gaster's *The Exempla of the Rabbis* and Haim Schwarzbaum's *Studies in Jewish and World Folklore*.

The complete story, "The Ant and the Impenetrable Palace," can be found in Micha Joseph Bin Gorion's *Mimekor Yisrael*.

"Story of the Ant" is in Nathan Ausubel's *A Treasury of Jewish Folklore*.

Motif: B 481.1—Helpful ant.

The Smell of Money

There are many legends about Solomon's wise and clever reasoning, which helped him to reach a just and fair decision in the court cases brought before him. Here is one of those stories.

HANNAH EARNED MONEY FOR HER FAMILY BY MAKING BROOMS. She gathered long stiff grass into a bundle, then tied the bundle to the end of a long stick to make a broom. She carried her brooms to the marketplace and stood there all day, selling them to earn a few coins.

At the end of the day, as she was walking home, she passed a bakery. "Oh," she thought. "Maybe I could spend one coin on something tasty." Then she decided, "No, my family needs the money. I'll just enjoy the smells and be on my way."

So Hannah stood outside the bakery door and smelled the freshly baked bread, the warm honey cake, and the sweet almond cookies.

The baker saw her at the door and grew suspicious. "What are you doing?" he asked her.

"I am smelling your delicious breads and cakes," she answered. "It's almost as good as eating it."

"Smelling my breads and cakes? You will have to pay for that." And he tried to grab her sack of coins.

"But I didn't eat anything," she cried. "I didn't eat them. I just smelled them."

Everyone in the market came rushing when they heard her. Some said the baker should be paid. Others said the girl owed nothing. They argued more and more until someone shouted out, "Ask the king. Let Solomon decide!"

So they took Hannah and the baker to King Solomon, the wisest king of all.

Solomon sat on his throne. "Speak," he said. "I will listen and I will judge."

The baker pointed his finger at Hannah and said, "That girl has to pay for what she took. I worked all day to make bread and cake and cookies. She stood at my door and smelled it all. It filled her with pleasure. She even admitted that it was practically as good as eating it."

"I should not have to pay," said Hannah. "The smell of the food was floating on the air. I only breathed the air. Do I have to pay to breathe?"

"Baker," said Solomon. "Do you care so much about money that you want to be paid even for the air around you?"

The baker answered, "The law says that you must pay if you take something that someone makes. She took the smells of the food that I made, so she must pay."

"That is the law," said Solomon. "The young woman must pay for what she took." Everyone in the crowd looked at each other in surprise.

"Young woman," said King Solomon, "take out your money."

So she did.

"Now shake the coins together in your hands."

She shook them once, twice, three times.

"Did you hear that?" said Solomon to the baker. "Now she has paid you."

"What do you mean?" he asked.

"She has paid for the smell of your breads and cakes with the sound of her money."

Hannah shook the coins again and again, and everybody else shook with laughter.

NOTE

A similar idea of finding an "appropriate" payment is found in a story told by Reb Nahman of Bratzlav (1770–1810), the great Hasidic storyteller who lived in Poland. The story is about a king who offers a reward to whoever can create the most beautiful picture on the wall of a great hall in the palace. One painter paints a wonderfully realistic picture of a garden. A second painter, who was always scheming to avoid doing any work, does not bother to paint anything. Instead he places a mirror on the opposite wall in such a way that it reflects the actual painting. The king must judge the two "pictures." First he places a bag of gold beside the actual painting and tells the first artist that this is his prize. Pointing to the reflection of the gold, he tells the second artist that the reflection is his reward. The lesson conveyed in this story is to know the difference between something that has worth and something that only appears to have worth but is not really worthy.

This Reb Nahman story is in *Kochavay Or*, and retold by Howard Schwartz and Barbara Rush as "The Royal Artists and the Clever King" in their book *A Coat for the Moon and Other Jewish Tales*. Interpreted as an allegorical tale, the king is a symbol for God. The endnote to the story states: "Thus on Yom Kippur God can look into our hearts and see clearly what reward we deserve" (81).

Another version of the artist with the mirror story is "The Reward," which can be found in Molly Cone's *Who Knows Ten?*

COMMENTARY

There are countless stories of wisdom, cleverness, and trickery told in *midrashim* as well as in legends and folktales. Some of these imaginative tales feature Biblical characters like Solomon and Elijah the Prophet, but no longer as the original biblical heroes. Instead, in folktales these characters become transformed as experts in a specific field. Solomon's domain is wisdom; Elijah the Prophet becomes the master of miracles.

While many legends tell about Solomon building the Temple in Jerusalem and how he accomplishes this great feat with the help of the demons, Solomon's main role, both as a young boy and as king, is as a wise judge.

Solomon, the son of King David and Bathsheba, lived in the tenth century B.C.E. and became the third king of Israel. He ruled over the land of Israel in a time of peace. His name in Hebrew, Shlomo, means *shalom*, "peace." He is known as the author of a great deal of wisdom literature, such as *Song of Songs*, *Proverbs*, and *Ecclesiastes*, and has been credited with being the creator of parables.

"The Smell of Money" is a well-known folktale in which Solomon is the judge who must decide what the fair amount would be for the "stolen" smells. In his clever way, he judges that the "sound" of money is the right kind of payment for the "smell" of cakes. One sense exchanged for another sense makes sense! In some versions of this story, the wise judge is the rabbi.

SOURCES AND VARIANTS

This is a universal tale that has been told in different ways in many countries. There are twenty Jewish versions of this tale from the East and West in the Israel Folktale Archives (IFA). Founded by the folklorist Dov Noy in 1955, this archive has gathered over twenty-three thousand folktales from the various ethnic communities in Israel and then classified them according to tale types and motifs.

IFA 4716 (Iraq) and IFA 1529 (Yemen) are two versions in the Israel Folktale Archives. The Iraqi story "The Beautiful Maiden and the Three Princes" was collected by Mukhtar Ezra from Yehezkel Danus (Baghdad) and published in Dov Noy's *Am Oved: Jewish-Iraqi Folktales*.

The Yemenite version is found in Dov Noy's *Jefet Schwili Tells: 195 Yemenite Folktales*, No. 96.

IFA 8990 (Morocco)—"The Cost of Meat."

IFA 9167 (Iraq)—"The Tale of a Cook and a Passer-By."

Jane Yolen includes a variant of this story from the African tradition in her anthology *Favorite Folktales from Around the World*. In this story, "Rich Man, Poor Man," originally published in Roger D. Abraham's *African Folktales*, 145–147, the poor man "steals" the smell of the rich man's meal and the payment is the bleating of a goat. In her endnote, Jane Yolen writes: "This African story is one variant of a popular wisdom tale that has been found as far away as Burma and Israel and throughout Europe." Rabelais published a version titled "The Theft of the Smell." In each version, payment is in a slightly different currency: in Burma the greedy stallkeeper gets paid with the shadow of a coin.

Still another version, "The Baker's Smell," which combines musical lyrics with narration, is composed and performed by Heather Forest on her *Songspinner* tape.

Tale Types: AT 1804B—Payment with the clink of money
AT 920-929—Clever acts and words
AT 926—Judgment of Solomon
AT 926C—Cases solved in a manner worthy of Solomon
Motifs: J 1172.2—Payment with the clink of money
J 1140—Clever judicial decisions

The Starling's Answer

Ancient legends say that Solomon was the only person since Adam and Eve who knew the languages of all creatures. The more Solomon understood the creatures in the world—the birds, beasts, and insects—the more respect and sympathy he had for them.
Here is a tale that shows not only the wisdom of a great king but also the wisdom of a simple bird.

KING SOLOMON'S WIFE HAD A PET STARLING THAT SHE TAUGHT TO sing. She kept it in a golden cage in a golden room of the palace. The starling had everything except one thing, and that was the only thing it really wanted.

One day, as Solomon walked by, the starling called to him, "Great King Solomon, may I ask you for a favor?"

King Solomon said, "What do you wish?"

"Freedom," said the bird.

Solomon shook his head, "I cannot set you free. You belong to my queen, not to me. However, I will tell her what you wish."

Solomon told the queen that the starling wanted freedom, but she said, "I love my starling's golden songs and shining dark feathers. How can I let it go? I will give it sweeter berries. I will give it a bigger cage. I will place it in a more beautiful room, but I will not set it free."

When the starling heard the queen's answer, it sang out, "Solomon, great King, grant me a different favor. I was taken from my nest as a baby. I have not met my mother or my father or any birds at all. Please tell another starling what my life is like and ask it how I can find my happiness."

"I will do that," said Solomon.

The next time Solomon went traveling, he remembered his promise. He was riding through a forest when he saw a starling flying overhead. He called out to it, "Little bird, I bring you greetings from a starling in my palace."

The bird landed on a nearby branch and listened carefully.

"Our starling sits in a golden cage, not in the branches of a tree. Its cage is in a walled garden, not in the open forest. It is given sweet berries but is not allowed to search for food. It is protected from all harm, but it cannot fly freely like you. It wants to know one thing, how can it find its happiness?"

The bird turned away as if it were thinking very deeply. A moment later, its head drooped, it shivered, then it fell to the ground. Solomon picked it up and warmed it in his hands. He blew gently on its face and sprinkled water on its beak. Still there was no sign of life. Sadly, Solomon placed it on the earth. He covered it with leaves and walked away.

As soon as Solomon returned to the palace, the pet starling fluttered inside its cage and sang out, "Did you find one of my kind? Did a brother or a sister bird say how I could find my happiness?"

"I asked but did not get an answer," said Solomon, and he told the bird what happened. "I found a starling in the forest and described your sad life. When I asked how you could find your happiness, the bird turned away. Its head drooped, it shivered, then it fell to the ground. I tried to help it, but all I could do was cover it with leaves and walk away."

The pet starling turned from Solomon and buried its head in its feathers. All that day it sat brooding, still and silent on its perch. It would not eat or drink. The next morning the queen saw it droop its head and shiver. It fell off its perch and landed on the bottom of the cage. The queen took it out and warmed it in her hands. She blew gently on its face and sprinkled water on its beak. She finally laid it in the garden and covered it with fallen leaves. She cried and said, "The poor bird has died from sadness. Oh, how I wish that I had set it free."

Then, just as she walked away, she heard a chirping that sounded like laughter. It was the starling, quite alive, fluttering out of the leaves, and as it did it said, "My dear princess, you're getting exactly what you wished for, and so am I!" It circled over her head and then upward past the high tower where Solomon was sitting.

"O great King Solomon, thank you for bringing me the answer from the bird in the forest. The bird was pretending to die. That was its message to me. So I pretended to die, and now, look, I'm free!" Off it flew, out of the palace, away from Jerusalem, over the hills of Judea toward the far-off forest of its family.

Solomon watched and smiled. He said, "I did not think the bird in the forest had answered my question, but the pet starling understood what I did not. Some answers are given without even a word being spoken."

NOTE

Solomon received this ability to understand the language of all living creatures as a young man. A legend relates that God visited Solomon in a dream and offered him a single wish. Solomon asked for a "listening heart." God was so pleased with this wish, that God granted Solomon "a heart that is wise and understanding" (I Kings 3:5–13). As a result, the forty-nine gates of wisdom opened to him. Out of one of those gates came the power to understand all languages, according to the Talmudic-midrashic tales. Solomon had other magical powers, such as the ability to fly on a magic carpet as well as on an eagle that carried him to faraway places, and the ability to talk to the winds.

A starling is a small black-and-brown speckled bird common in Europe and the Middle East. It imitates sounds like a parrot, and it can be trained to sing.

COMMENTARY

A similar type of action that is meant to be interpreted by the seeker of advice is in a Talmudic *agada*. The emperor Antoninus sent a messenger to Rabbi Yehuda Ha-Nasi for advice about how to save the dwindling royal treasury. Hearing the request, the rabbi did not respond with words but only dug up the large vegetables in his garden and replaced them with small vegetables. When the messenger told the emperor about this curious activity, he understood what he had to do. The emperor dismissed his chief tax collectors and other officials of the court and replaced them with honest officials. This story, "Advice and Hints: A Tale of Antoninus and Rabbi Judah," is in Micha Joseph Bin Gorion's *Mimekor Yisrael Vol. II*. Another version, "How to Replenish a Treasury," can be found in Nathan Ausubel's *A Treasury of Jewish Folklore*.

SOURCES AND VARIANTS

One of the earliest Jewish sources for this story is in Berechiah ha-Nakdan's *Mishle Shu'alim* (Fox Fables), a medieval text. In this twelfth-century French book, the story revolves around a knight and a lady instead of Solomon and his wife. The bird flies away without any explanation. This story also appears in *The Arabian Nights*.

"The Starling and the Princess," in Ellen Frankel's *The Classic Tales: 4,000 Years of Jewish Lore*.

"The Parrot's Advice," in Pinhas Sadeh's *Jewish Folktales*, which is about a princess, her slave, and her captive parrot.

Motif: K 522.4—Captive parrots in net play dead and are thrown out; escape

Solomon's Ring of Wisdom

What if you were allowed only three or four words that would be an answer to the world's greatest problem or that would give a perspective when one is too filled with pride or arrogance or too filled with uncertainty and sadness. In this story, Benaiah, identified as King Solomon's trusted lieutenant or servant, seeks the greatest wisdom to offer him.

LATE ONE NIGHT, BENAIAH, THE MOST TRUSTED SERVANT OF KING Solomon, saw Solomon sitting wearily on his throne with his head bowed in the darkness. "Something is troubling my king," Benaiah thought. Then he saw Solomon take off his ring, the great Ring of Power that held four magic jewels. Each jewel had been given to Solomon by a different angel with a different power. Each jewel was engraved with a sacred letter. Together those four letters spelled the most powerful name of the many secret names of God.

Solomon had great powers. He knew all the languages of all living beings. He could command the wind and water. The ring gave him even greater powers, though only Solomon knew what those powers were.

Solomon raised his head and gazed at Benaiah standing in the doorway. "I am not worthy of this ring," he said.

"Why not?" asked Benaiah.

"Sometimes when I fail, I feel beaten down by uncertainty. Then I become afraid to use my power. Sometimes when I succeed, I feel puffed up with pride. Then I become reckless and I misuse my power."

Benaiah wanted to say that Solomon had never made mistakes and had never acted foolishly, but he knew it was not true, not even for the wisest king in the world.

"Can anything help you, great King?" he asked.

Solomon said, "When I become unsure of myself, I need to be comforted. When I become too sure of myself, I need to be warned."

"Let me stay at your side," said Benaiah. "When you feel too low and weak, I will comfort you. When you act too high and mighty, I will warn you," said Benaiah.

Solomon smiled sadly and shook his head. Benaiah was a good and loyal servant, but they both knew that he was not wise enough to comfort or to warn the king.

"Let me help in another way," said Benaiah. "Let me find the greatest words of wisdom that will help you."

"Go, Benaiah," said Solomon. "It is what you wish and what I need."

Benaiah bowed and left the palace. He traveled throughout the land questioning the wisest men and women. He asked each one, "When failure makes the king feel too low and weak, what words will comfort him?" Everyone had a different answer, and every answer was good and wise in one way or another. Benaiah also asked, "When success makes the king feel too high and mighty, what words will warn him?" Again, all the answers were different, but each answer had some value. Benaiah wrote down every word. Finally he reached the Dead Sea, where no one lived. He had traveled through the entire land.

Benaiah gazed at all the words of wisdom he had gathered. The words filled many pages, the pages filled many books, the books filled many boxes. "Too many words," Benaiah thought. "How can the king read all these words each time he needs comfort or warning?" Benaiah left it all behind, and he headed back to the palace empty-handed.

When he reached the high gates of Jerusalem, he lost heart and sank to the ground. "I have failed," he said, staring at the dust. He felt so low and weak that he could not do anything but listen to the birds chirping in the sky. He could not understand them as Solomon could, but he could imagine what they were saying.

"Failure, failure," they seemed to sing as they circled overhead. He nodded sadly and said, "It's true. I have failed terribly." Then he heard the wind passing through the trees, and he imagined that it was whispering to him, "This . . . too . . . shall . . . pass. This . . . too . . . shall . . . pass."

"It's true," he thought. "This is an awful time for me, but this, too, shall pass." Benaiah felt comforted.

Suddenly, Benaiah jumped to his feet. "That is what I will say to Solomon! I will say, 'This, too, shall pass!' Those words will help him just as they helped me!"

Benaiah felt proud of himself. He had succeeded after all. He strutted high and mighty through the gate toward the palace. Now the birds above him seemed to be singing, "Success! Success!"

Benaiah bragged out loud, "I asked all the wisest men and women. None of them knew what to say, but I found the perfect words." He was walking tall and all puffed up with pride. "Solomon will praise me. Everybody will admire me."

Then he heard the wind whispering again as it flowed over the rooftops and around the palace towers. "This . . . too . . . shall . . . pass."

Benaiah stopped and listened to the warning of the wind. He sighed, "It's true. Today I am a great success, but tomorrow I may fail again. I feel high and mighty now, but this, too, shall pass."

Benaiah walked slowly into the palace. Everyone rushed to hear the wisdom he had brought, but he said nothing until he stood before King Solomon's throne. Then he announced, "Great King,

I have heard wise words from all the wisest men and women in the land, but nothing that they said was wise enough. The wisest words that I have found were carried by the wind, for the wind passes over everything both high and low, and it has seen all things at their best and all things at their worst. The wind flowed over me and over this great city even higher than the towers of this palace, and it whispered these words, "This, too, shall pass."

The nobles, the servants, and guards said to one another, "Those are such simple words. Why does Benaiah think that they are special?"

Solomon smiled. He descended from his throne and embraced his servant. "Benaiah, you have brought me the wisdom that I needed. These words are a comfort and a warning to us all."

Solomon had a ring made to match his Ring of Power. He called it his Ring of Wisdom. It was not made of shining gold like his other ring. Instead, it was made of soft and common copper that turned dark on his finger. He did not decorate it with precious jewels. Instead he engraved the ring with the first letters of these words, "This, Too, Shall Pass."

NOTES

In the Night Prayer, recited before going to sleep, there is a reference to the four angels who gave Solomon the magic Ring of Power. "In the name of the Lord God of Israel, may Michael be at my right hand and Gabriel at my left; before me, Uriel; behind me, Raphael; and above my head, the divine presence." These angels stood guard around Solomon at the four corners of his bed. The names of these four angels—Raphael, Uriel, Michael, and Gabriel—comprise different aspects of El, which is one of the many names of God. "The archangel Michael appeared to him, and gave him a small ring having a seal consisting of an engraved stone, and he said to him: 'Take, O Solomon, king, son of David, the gift which the Lord God . . . hath sent unto thee. With it thou shalt lock up all the demons of the earth, male and female; and with their help thou shalt build up Jerusalem. But thou must wear this seal of God. . . . " (Ginzberg IV:150).

Among the many legends of Solomon, some show how the Ring of Power gave Solomon control over demons and their secrets. By having this power, Solomon was able to order the demons to help build the Temple of Jerusalem, because he wanted all creatures both high and low to take part in its creation. He also was able to use this power to overpower his antagonist, Ashmodai, the King of the Demons, and trick Ashmodai into giving him the magical Shamir worm, created at twilight on the sixth day of Creation. Solomon needed this Shamir, which had the unique power to cut through stone. Then he was able to use the Shamir to cut through the stone quarry in order to build the altar, since no iron tools, which are associated with war, could be used for the holy temple dedicated to God.

The words "This, too, shall pass" translate into the three Hebrew words "Gam Ze Ya'avor." It is represented by the letters Gimel, Zayin, and Yud. Some young American Jews who left home to fight in World War II were given these "good luck" rings with those three Hebrew letters engraved on them.

COMMENTARY

These magical words have helped people I know, especially when they were going through traumatic times. They can help create a balance in our lives when we get overprideful, or even overjoyed, as well as overupset. A value in Judaism is to achieve a balance in our lives.

I recall one version where Solomon decides to trick Benaiah into going on a fool's errand. He sends his loyal and always-successful lieutenant to find a ring that will make a happy man sad and a sad man happy. Benaiah searches and finally finds a jeweler who engraves the words "*Gam Ze Ya'avor*" on a ring.

On Benaiah's return, Solomon is laughing with glee at what he had done, certain that Benaiah would have failed at this impossible task. But when Solomon sees the ring, his laughter evaporates, and he suddenly realizes the power of these words to make a happy man sad and a sad man happy. It was a sobering experience for this usually wise king.

SOURCES AND VARIANTS

Louis Ginzberg's *The Legends of the Jews*, Vol. IV, 150–169, and Vol. VI, 292.

"King Solomon's Ring" in Judith Ish-Kishor's *Tales from the Wise Men of Israel*.

IFA 126 from Turkey. "This Too Will Pass," recorded by Heda Jason as told by D. Franco. In Dov Noy's *Folktales of Israel*, No. 63.

IFA 7904 from Morocco. "Two Brothers," recorded by Aliza Ohayon as told by her father Yosef Ohayon in *A Tale for Each Month 1967*, edited by Edna Cheichal. In this tale, "Two Brothers," a man suggests to his brother that he sell him as a slave, because they are starving. One day the man visited his slave brother and found him rich. To his surprise, the rich brother tells him that he inherited his master's wealth, and says to him, "This, too, will pass." On another occasion, this rich brother becomes a king and again tells the surprised brother, "This, too, will pass." On the third meeting, the rich brother is ill, and he then says, "All passed, my brother, but this will not pass."

Tale type: AT 910*Q—This, too, will pass
Motifs: H86.3—Ring with names inscribed on it
D1317.5—Magic ring gives warning
D1500.1.8—Magic amulet cures disease

Enough

Solomon was the last of the great kings. The kings who followed him lost the respect of the people. Prophets became the true leaders of Israel. They inspired the people, guiding them and criticizing them if necessary. They even criticized the kings, which could be dangerous. Many call Elijah the greatest of all the prophets.

King Solomon may have been the wisest man in the world, but Elijah's wisdom came from another world. He was a seer and a miracle worker more powerful than all the wizards who tried to defeat him and more fiercely outspoken than any prophet. It is said that Elijah never died. Instead, God sent a cosmic chariot, and Elijah rose to Heaven in a fiery blast.

People loved to tell stories of the prophet Elijah returning in disguise. He tempts and tests people. He is not fooled by clever words or crafty deeds; so if they are up to no good, Elijah will know and he will show them a trick or two, as he does in this tale.

A POOR YOUNG MAN AND HIS YOUNG WIFE WERE CELEBRATING the Passover holiday with the best meal they could manage. They raised their glasses to wish for a better future in a better world, and just then, there was a knock at the door. A traveling beggar stood outside with his hand outstretched, saying nothing.

They told him, "You are welcome here. Please join us. We don't have much to eat or drink, but we have a wonderful story that we can share with you." They shared their food and drink, and they shared the story of Passover: the story of how their ancestors had been slaves in Egypt and how they had been freed to seek the Promised Land.

The three of them stayed up late that night describing the wonders of that time: how Moses ran from Egypt but stopped his running when he found a burning bush that told him, "Go back!"

They counted the ten catastrophes that struck Egypt until the pharaoh let the people go, and they sang about how the people found their freedom. Finally, the candles were burning out, and there were no more candles left to light.

"Please stay," they told the traveler. "You can sleep in our bed, and we will make ourselves a bed of hay."

"Thank you for all your kindness, but I must continue on my journey," said the traveler. As he headed out the door, he smiled warmly and said, "May the next thing you do have no end until you say, 'Enough!'" Then he was gone.

"He will need money on his journey," said the wife. She reached into her pocket for the only money they had, a silver coin. When she took it out she felt another coin in her pocket. She took that one out and felt another. No matter how many coins she took out, there was always one more in her pocket. She piled the table high with silver coins until they were spilling over and covering the floor.

The wife said, "We have all the money we will ever need."

"You are right," said the husband. "It's enough." The moment he said the word "Enough," there were no more coins in her pocket. The magic was over. The two of them sat down and stared at their great fortune.

"That was no ordinary man," said his wife. "That must have been the prophet Elijah in disguise."

At that moment there was another knock at the door. Had Elijah returned? They rushed to open the door, but instead of Elijah, there stood the husband's hardhearted brother and his brother's hard-hearted wife. They had come to collect the rent.

The rich brother was amazed at all the coins. "Where did you get that money?" he asked.

They answered, "It was a gift from the prophet Elijah. We shared the little that we had, and he gave us all of this." They told them the whole story.

"Where is Elijah now?" asked the rich brother.

"He is walking down the road," they said.

The rich brother and his wife rushed to their carriage and whipped the horses into a mad gallop. They caught up to Elijah and called out, "Sir, you must be tired. Come rest in our home."

Elijah refused, but they kept insisting until finally he agreed, and they took him back to their home. The rich brother showed Elijah his huge house, saying, "My mansion is better than my poor brother's little shack." Elijah looked at the many rooms with marble floors and fancy furniture, but he was not impressed.

The wife ordered the servants to serve the finest foods. She said, "This dinner is better than their poor scraps of food." Elijah hardly ate anything.

They brought in a band of musicians to play. "Our music is better than their singing!" they said. Then the rich brother and his wife told stories, but not the Passover story about their ancestors who were slaves in Egypt. They only talked about themselves. They bragged about how they had become so rich and important. Elijah said nothing.

Finally, they said, "We'll show you to your bed."

"No," said Elijah. "I must continue on my journey."

"Then, here is some money," said the rich brother, and he slyly gave him five gold coins. "Now what are you going to give us in return?"

"What do you want?" asked Elijah.

The rich brother said, "We want more than you gave my brother and his wife. After all, we gave you more than they did."

Elijah replied, "You gave me less than they did because you gave nothing out of kindness."

"We still deserve something," they both said.

"Yes, you do deserve something," he said. "So I will give you what I gave them. May the next thing you do have no end until you say, 'Enough!'" He walked out the door, and when they looked for him, he was nowhere to be seen.

The rich brother rushed back inside and was about to grab his money box so he could pull out a large gold coin. "Wait," said the wife. "Let's be sure no one sees what we are doing. You close the front door, and I'll shutter the front window."

He shut the door, and she closed the shutters of the window. "Good!" she said. "Now let's fill the house with gold!"

But suddenly she found herself opening the shutters again and closing them with a bang. The husband found himself opening the door again and slamming it shut. And again. And again.

"I can't stop!" cried the husband.

"Neither can I!" cried the wife. "We have to say the word your brother said."

"No!" the husband yelled. "That will end the magic, and we'll lose our chance to make a fortune. We have to think of something else."

However, they could not think of anything else or do anything else. So on and on they went, slamming the door and banging the shutters. All the neighbors heard the racket and saw what they were doing. Soon everyone in town came to look and laugh at the richest, most important man and woman slamming their door and shutting their shutters. The two of them would not and could not stop all day and all night long until the sun came up and they finally gave up. Together they called out, "Enough!" The spell broke, and they fell backward into the house exhausted as everybody clapped and laughed. They were so upset that they stayed inside for weeks, and when they finally did come out they never dared to brag to anyone again. They'd had enough.

NOTES

The time period in this story is the Passover holiday in spring that looks back on the time when the Jewish people were freed from slavery in Egypt and recalls their journey to the Promised Land. It is celebrated in the home with a ceremonial meal called a *seder*. The family reads from a book called the *Haggadah*, which leads them through the story and the rituals and blessings that happen during the meal. Certain foods at the table symbolize the Passover experience: a hard-boiled egg represents the sacrifices made at the Temple, bitter herbs express the suffering of slavery, nuts mixed in honey represents the cement used to build the pharaoh's cities, greens symbolize the spring, and ten drops of wine symbolize the ten plagues that finally forced the pharaoh to free the Jews. Flat unleavened bread called *matza* is eaten during the ten days of the holiday because the Jews had to rush out of Egypt without having time for their bread to rise. Everyone has a role in the ceremonial meal, especially children. They ask four ritual questions, and they find the hidden matza, which they "sell" to the host for a ransom in order for the seder to continue.

Near the end of the seder, the door is opened for the prophet Elijah, who enters invisibly and "drinks" from a special cup of wine placed on the table in his honor. Then everyone calls out, "Next year in Jerusalem!" This is the great wish of the Jewish people, to return to the Promised Land.

COMMENTARY

Elijah in the Bible is a "fire and brimstone" type of prophet and identified as the forerunner of the Messiah. However, as a folklore hero, Elijah the Prophet, may he be remembered for good, is a sympathetic, caring hero who brings hope and miracles to the deserving and hospitable poor people. Actually, Elijah the Prophet is the most popular acting hero in all of Jewish folklore: in folktales, folksongs, life-cycle rituals, and in prayers and blessings around the year/month/week/day cycle. He is mentioned in the grace after meals as well as at *Havdalah* at the end of the Sabbath.

Elijah the Prophet is also a master of disguise, since he shows up in most stories as a mysterious character, for example, as a magician, a beggar, an old man, or even a handsome young man. Since one never knows who Elijah the Prophet is, or how he will appear, the fascination we have had for him for thousands of years, through every generation, continues. Since he never died, but was lifted in a fiery chariot to Heaven, Elijah continues to live in our imaginations, our tales, our rituals, and our songs.

The source of "Foolish Wishes" may be 2 Kings 4:1–7, which is the story of Elisha, Elijah's disciple, and the widow's oil. The blessing "May what you do be blessed until you say 'Enough!'" is illustrated in this message in the Second Book of Kings.

SOURCES AND VARIANTS

This story of the rich brother and the poor brother is found in Louis Ginzberg's *The Legends of the Jews*, IV:211–212, as well as in Moses Gaster's *Exempla of the Rabbis*, No. 435. These are Jewish versions of a tale that was widespread among many nations, but especially popular among German Jews.

In the Israel Folktale Archives there are many versions: IFA 49 (Turkey), 195 (Samaritan), 384 (Tunis), 437 (Peki'in Village), 829 (Aleppo), 879 (Palestinian, Sephardi), 960 (Poland), 1038 (Eastern Europe), 1053 and 1065 (Morocco), 1229 and 1313 (Egypt), and 2922 (Eastern Europe).

An old version of this tale can be found in *Mishle Sindbad*.

Another version can be found in Eliezer Shteinman's *Kitve ha-Maggid mi-Dubno*. In the Dubner Maggid version, a rabbi bestows the blessing upon a traveler to continue doing all day what he first does upon arriving home. When his wife refuses to get the money to count, they begin to quarrel. As a consequence, they keep on quarreling all day and all night.

Other sources for variants include *Sefer ha-Bhiha veha-Hiddud*; Abraham Tendlau's *Spruchworter und Redensarten deutsch-judischer Vorzeit*; Theodor Benfrey's *Pantscantantra; Sihot Hayim*; Immanuel Olsvanger's *Rosinkes mit Mandlen*; M. Ben-Yehezkel's *The Book of Tales*; Dov Noy's *Folktales of Israel*; Haim Schwarzbaum's *Studies in Jewish and World Folklore*, with extensive notes on 241–245; and the fables of Aesop and Marie de France.

A version of this story, "A Beggar's Blessing," is in Peninnah Schram's *Tales of Elijah the Prophet* (197–199), with notes on pages 282–283.

Tale types: AT 750A—The wishes
AT 750B—Hospitality rewarded
AT 565—The magic mill

Motifs: D 1720.1—Man given power of wishing

D 2100.1—Inexhaustible treasure

D 2172.2—Magic gift: power to continue all day what one starts

H 1564—Test of hospitality

J 2071—A limited number of wishes will be fulfilled

J 2073.1—Wise and foolish wish: keep doing all day what you begin

J 2415—Foolish imitation of lucky man

K 1811.3—Saint in disguise [Elijah] visits mortal

Q 1.1—Saint in disguise [Elijah] rewards hospitality

Q 286.1—Uncharitableness to holy person punished

Q 42.3—Generosity to saint in disguise [Elijah] rewarded

Golden Plates

The Prophet Elijah is described in the Bible as strict and demanding. He expected proper behavior from both beggars and kings. However, the folktales created by ordinary folk described him as loving and generous, someone who found clever ways to reward and punish people.

In this story, adapted and expanded from one told by the Jews of Turkey, Elijah was impressed by a young girl's intelligence as well as by her decent nature. They have a gentle battle of wits and wills, and they both get exactly what they want.

DEVORAH WAS ONLY SIXTEEN YEARS OLD WHEN HER PARENTS DIED. Since she was blind, she could not find work. Since she had no one to care for her, she was told to go to the marketplace to beg. However, Devorah would not beg. Instead, she sang.

She didn't sing perfectly, she didn't even sing loudly, but she sang with such pure feeling that everyone stopped to listen, and those who could tossed a coin into her cup. Devorah sang the songs she loved the most: working songs, lullabies, and the sacred songs that her people sang on the Sabbath and the Holy Days.

One day she heard a stranger say in a gruff voice, "Young woman, you are singing the wrong songs in the wrong place for the wrong reason."

Devorah might have ignored the stranger, or she might have told him to go away, but he sounded so wise and so mysterious that she fell silent. She felt that the stranger had not come from another land but from another world.

She was right. This was the prophet Elijah, whose spirit returns at times in disguise. He had come to test her.

"I am not doing anything wrong," she told him.

"Prove it by answering a question," he said.

"I will," she said.

Elijah asked his question: "Is it right to sing sacred songs for money in a marketplace?"

"I sing to live, and I live to sing," she answered. "The Creator who gave me the right to live is the One who gave me the right to sing."

Elijah smiled at her intelligent reply, but his voice remained serious. "You have answered only the first part of my question. Sacred songs are sung in a synagogue or at home when friends and family gather to pray. What gives you the right to sing them in the marketplace, where people come to buy and sell?"

"Where else can I sing?" she answered. "This is the only home I have, and these people are my only family and friends."

Elijah nodded, for he knew that her songs made the people happy. He said, "You still have not answered the last part of my question. Sacred songs are sung to thank the Creator. What gives you the right to sing those songs for money?"

Devorah answered, "If I am doing wrong, let the Creator who took my eyesight take my voice as well."

Elijah laughed softly and said, "Young woman, you are as pure as your songs." He gently touched her cheek, and as soon as he touched her, she could sense that he was no ordinary person.

Then he said, "I will grant you one wish."

Devorah thought deeply and imagined her heart's deepest desire. A moment later her face brightened. She sang out:

"Blindness, loneliness, poverty
are my three fates.
I wish to see my children eat
from golden plates."

Elijah laughed out loud. "Devorah, you have wished for sight, children, and wealth," he said, "You are trying to get three gifts from one wish."

"It is true," she said. "But you asked me one question: Is it right to sing sacred songs for money in a marketplace? That one question required three answers. It's only fair that my one wish should give me three gifts."

This time Elijah laughed a full and hearty laugh. He said, "You have now made me laugh three times, so I will make you happy in three ways."

So it was. Devorah's sight returned. She married and had three children. Devorah's good fortune grew as quickly as her children. She became so wealthy that she was able to see her children eat from golden plates.

NOTES

Even a prophet's mind could be changed by a convincing argument. Discussion was always important in Jewish learning. It is not enough to learn the stories and the laws. And it is not enough to be told what they mean. We must decide what they mean for ourselves. That requires study, discussion, even disagreement and debate, and especially questions. Here's an example from a two-thousand-year-old story, "The Law Is No Longer in Heaven."

Two great scholars, Rabbi Eliezer ben Hyrcanos and Rabbi Yoshua, as well as other sages, were disagreeing about the meaning of a religious law. (Eliezer ben Hyracanos lived at the end of the first century into the beginning of the second century.) Yoshua wanted all the great scholars to decide by voting. Instead, Eliezer called out to God, "If I am right, let the carob tree uproot itself and move one hundred cubits." It did. The scholars still disagreed. Eliezer said, "If I am right let the water in the canal flow backward." It did. They still disagreed. Eliezer said, "If I am right, let the walls of the study house collapse." The walls began to bend, and Yoshua called out, "God, don't get involved. You gave us the laws at Mount Sinai. You told us to study them and decide how to live them. The laws are no longer in heaven; they are here on Earth for us to interpret." Hence, in deference to Rabbi Yoshua, the walls did not fall. And in deference to Rabbi Eliezer, the walls did not resume their upright position. They are still standing at a slant.

When Rabbi Nathan met Elijah the Prophet and asked him, "What did the Holy One do in that moment?" Elijah replied, "He laughed with joy, saying, 'My children have prevailed over Me. My children have prevailed over Me.'" (Babyonian Talmud, Bava Mezia, 59b).

Ellen Frankel includes "The Law Is Not in Heaven" in her anthology, *The Classic Tales: 4,000 Years of Jewish Lore*. The final line in her translation is "My children have gotten the better of Me! My children have bested Me."

COMMENTARY

The core of this story is based on a Turkish folktale: An old blind man who is poor as well as childless encounters Elijah the Prophet. Elijah tells him, "God sees your poverty and has pity on you, and He is willing to help you. How do you want God to help you?" He also tells him that he will have only one wish. The old man asks his wife what to wish for, then returns to tell Elijah his three-in-one wish. Usually, as in so many of the Elijah tales, Elijah gives a reward to a good person by saying, "I will grant you one wish" (or even more sometimes). However, in this tale, it is unusual that Elijah has God as the one to grant the wish. In this sense, Elijah, as an angel that he may actually be, becomes the intermediary.

There is a great deal of mystery surrounding the identity of Elijah the Prophet. Since there is no family lineage given in the Torah for this prophet, he seems to be an angel sent as a messenger from God to right injustices and bring hope to people. He appears and disappears, then reappears, often in disguise. In the folktales, Elijah is the hero who serves as intermediary between Heaven and Earth, helper, teacher, guide, miracle maker. He always aids the worthy and hospitable protagonist to reach his or her goals.

Most of the Elijah stories are religious tales with an intended message or moral that needs to be learned and integrated into one's life. These tales often have as their main purpose the teaching of values and faith in God; they embody a *musar haskl*, an ethical lesson. However, these tales go beyond mere moralizing. As a matter of fact, many motifs that can also be found in secular folktales are blended into these pious tales. These narratives serve to entertain and inspire. They not only bring hope but also give people a perspective of "This, too, shall pass." These tales allow people to express their wishes and prayers through words and to help them bear persecutions or relieve tensions from blood-libel accusations. They help people endure poverty and other problems. The tales are there in times when people need a good, compassionate angel. (For more on Elijah the Prophet, see the foreword by Dov Noy and the introduction by Peninnah Schram in her *Tales of Elijah the Prophet*.)

SOURCES AND VARIANTS

I have not found any version of this tale that involves a blind girl. I believe that the reteller of this story created this variation, which expresses such a beautiful philosophy about a young woman singing sacred songs, even in a marketplace.

The wish segment is based on the Jewish Turkish tale (IFA 12578) collected in the late 1950s by Kamelia Shakhar-Russo. The woman who told the story had heard it from her grandmother in Izmir, Turkey. It was published in Hebrew by Dov Noy and Tamar Alexander, co-editors, in *The Treasure of Our Fathers, Judeo-Spanish Tales*.

A translated version of this story appears in English (translated by Stephen Levy) in Howard Schwartz's anthology *Gates to the New City* as "The Poor Man and Eliyahu the Prophet."

A version of this story, "Elijah and the Poor Man's Wish," is in *Circle Spinning: Jewish Turning and Returning Tales*, by Cherie Karo Schwartz.

Tale type: AT 920-929D—Clever acts and words. This wish request segment is a clever variation of "One wish that includes other wishes."

Motifs: J 1280—Wise answers to a king or judge.

K 1811.3—Saint in disguise [Elijah] visits mortal

N 202—Wishes for good fortune realized

The Seven Questions of Alexander the Great

Israel was never as powerful as the large warrior nations of the world. Its true power was in its beliefs. Larger nations invaded and dominated it. The Jewish people survived by holding on to their beliefs.

Here is a tale of one of those invaders and how the leaders of Israel were able to impress him with their beliefs, showing him that wisdom can be greater than force.

ALEXANDER THE GREAT OF MACEDONIA WAS THE GREATEST warrior of the ancient world. He conquered all the lands from North Africa to India. In 333 B.C.E., he led his army into Jerusalem and demanded to meet the wisest of all the Jews.

When the Wise Ones arrived, Alexander told them, "I love wisdom above everything. If you answer all my questions, I will let you go in peace."

The Wise Ones were silent. They knew that he did not love wisdom above everything else. They had heard what Alexander did when he entered the land of Gordia. The Gordians brought Alexander a rope that had been cleverly knotted into a very complicated ball. They told him, "Whoever wants to be king of Gordia must be able to free this rope from all its knots. Are you wise enough?"

Alexander drew his sword and said," I am powerful enough!" He slashed the ball of rope to bits, and he declared, "I have freed the rope from all its knots. I am now king of Gordia."

The Wise Ones of Jerusalem understood that Alexander loved power more than wisdom. They knew they had to be careful how they answered his questions.

Alexander asked them, "Who is wise?"

They answered, "Those who can see all the effects of their actions."

"Who is a hero?"

"Those who can conquer their own fears and desires."

"Who is rich?"

"Those who are satisfied with what they have."

"How can a person earn friends?"

"By not trying to have more power than others."

Alexander became angry. He said, "That's not true. I have more power than anyone else in the whole world. Many people become my friends because I have the power to help them."

The Wise Ones were silent. Alexander could see that the Wise Ones believed that those people would not be true friends.

Alexander asked, "Who is the wisest among you?"

They answered, "We are equally wise."

"If you are all wise, then why don't you follow my beliefs and act as I do? Don't you respect me?"

"We are always being tempted to change our beliefs and act like others, but we give our highest respect to those who resist temptation."

Alexander then became very angry. He said, "I can say a single word, and my guards will kill you all. Why are you not afraid!"

They answered, "We are not afraid because you promised that if we answered your questions, you would let us go in peace. A king with your great power would not lie."

Alexander realized that he had to let them go or he would look like a liar. He overcame his anger and said, "You have spoken with great wisdom." He gave them gifts of gold and silver, and he let them go in peace.

NOTES

Gordia was an ancient kingdom in west-central Asia Minor, in what is now Turkey, settled in the thirteenth century B.C.E. The Gordian knot was an intricate knot tied by King Gordius of Phrygia and cut (in a shortcut way to solve the problem) by Alexander the Great with his sword after hearing an oracle promise that whoever could undo the knot would be the next ruler of Asia. The term "Gordian knot" has come to mean an exceedingly complicated problem.

Alexander the Great (356–323 B.C.E.) was the king of Macedonia, an ancient kingdom north of Greece. He conquered Greece, the Persian Empire, and Egypt. Alexander the Great was mentioned extensively in Talmudic, midrashic, and medieval Jewish legends. He treated the Jews with respect. To honor him, many Jewish children were named Alexander or Alexandra.

However, Alexander the Great also introduced Greek culture and beliefs into the region. This created a problem a century or so later. The Syrians, who had accepted Greek culture, occupied Israel and demanded that the Jews worship Greek gods as they did. They placed an idol of Zeus in the Temple and ordered Jews to bow down to it and also sacrifice pigs to it. Anyone who refused was killed. Many gave up their lives.

This was a time when wisdom was not enough. The people had to use force to defend their beliefs. The Maccabee family led a rebellion in 167 B.C.E. The enemy was driven out, and the Temple was restored. However, only a small amount of sacred oil was left to light the Temple's *menorah* (lamp). But, according to legend, a miracle occurred, and the menorah burned for eight days. This was long enough to produce more sacred oil and keep the Temple lamp burning without interruption.

These events are celebrated on Hanukkah, which usually falls in December. Each Jewish home has a Hanukkiah (Hanukkah lamp). Sometimes each family member has his or her own. While the Hanukkiah has places for nine candles, eight candles represent the eight days and nights that the Temple lamp burned. The ninth candle is the *shamash* (helper), which is used to light the other candles. The candles are lit in sequence, beginning with one candle on the first night, then two on the second night, until the eighth night when the entire Hannukiah is lit.

The holiday is celebrated with parties and gifts. A favorite game uses a *dreidel* (a spinning top with four sides). Each side of the dreidel has a Hebrew letter. The letters stand for the words "A Great Miracle Happened There."

This recalls the time when the Greeks did not allow Jews to gather to study their religion. People who gathered to study would spin a dreidel so that the soldiers would think they were just gambling.

SOURCES AND VARIANTS
The story can be found in the Babylonian Talmud, Tamid 31b–32a. It is also found in Bialik and Ravnitzky's *The Book of Legends*. Here you will find that Alexander put ten questions to the elders of the Negev, the south country. According to historical accounts, Alexander the Great had actually visited the land of Israel. The other questions were: Which is farther—from Heaven to Earth or from east to west? Was Heaven created first, or the Earth? Was light created first, or darkness?

Many folktales, along with *aggadot* and *midrashim*, revolve around questions and riddles. The cleverness of the answers often reveals how Jews use wisdom from the sacred texts as well as non-linear logical approaches to the questions. To illustrate, listen to the responses by the elders for the first two questions stated above: "From east to west. The proof is that when the sun is in the east, [it is so far away that] all can look at it; but when the sun is in the middle of the sky, [it is so close that] no one can look at it"; and "Heaven was created first, as Scripture says, 'In the beginning God created the heavens and then the earth'" (Genesis 1:2) (*The Book of Legends*, 167).

Tale Types: AT 920A*—The inquisitive king
AT 922*C—Jew(s) requested to answer questions or perform task

Who Knows?

Akiva lived in Israel in the first century C.E. He was a poor shepherd who could not read or write. However, when he was forty years old, he married a young woman, Rachel, who believed in him and convinced him to get an education. Akiva studied Torah and became the greatest teacher in the land.

The Romans ruled Judea at the time. They decided that the best way to control the people was to destroy their beliefs. The Romans made it illegal to teach or learn anything about being Jewish. The punishment was death.

Akiva continued to teach. Someone named Rabbi Pappus Ben Yehuda asked him, "Why do you keep teaching Jewish beliefs? The Romans will kill you."

Akiva answered with a story. "The fish in a river were trying to escape a net. A sly fox called to them, 'It's dangerous in the water. Jump out. You'll be safe on the land.' The fish answered, 'We'll stay here. We have a better chance of surviving in the water than on the land.' "

"Why did you tell me that story?" Ben Yehudah asked Akiva.

Akiva answered, "The story is a parable. We Jews are like those fish. Fish cannot survive without water, and we cannot survive without our beliefs."

Akiva traveled the land teaching whoever dared to learn. Here is a story of one thing that he taught.

AKIVA AND BEN YEHUDAH WERE TRAVELING BY HORSE ACROSS THE country. It was late at night when they finally reached a walled town surrounded by a forest. They called to the guard, "Open the gate."

"You are strangers," said the guard. "And you have come too late. The gate is locked for the night."

Akiva said, "There is nowhere else to stay, and we hear there are bandits nearby."

"Perhaps you are bandits," said the guard. "Perhaps you are trying to trick me into opening the gate." He aimed an arrow at Akiva and shouted, "Go away."

Akiva and Ben Yehudah turned and rode off. "We will have to sleep outside. This is bad," said Ben Yehudah.

Akiva said, "Who knows what good may come from this? Let's just say, 'It is for the best.' "

Ben Yehudah frowned. He looked at the dark forest all around them. He lit his lantern to search for a place to camp near the road.

He saw a cave, but when they came near, a lion leaped out. It roared and attacked the horses. Akiva and Ben Yehudah were thrown to the ground. The lantern broke, and the horses galloped away as the lion chased after them. Akiva and Ben Yehuda ran deep into the woods and climbed a high tree for protection.

"We don't dare camp near the road now," said Ben Yehudah. "This is very bad."

"Who knows?" said Akiva. "This, too, can be for the best." Ben Yehudah only shook his head and said nothing.

Just as the rain ended, they heard the sound of horses. They saw riders in the distance carrying flaming torches. "Those riders can help us," said Ben Yehudah. He climbed down the tree and ran toward the riders, calling for them to stop; but they were too far away to hear him, and they rode out of sight.

"I couldn't stop them. We'll have to stay here all night," said Ben Yehudah. "This is as bad as it can get."

"Who knows?" said Akiva, "Even this, too, can be for the best."

This time Ben Yehudah glared angrily and kicked a stone. "There can't be anything good about this!" he growled, and he would not listen to another word.

In the morning, cold and hungry, they trudged down the road looking for their horses. The road led them toward the walled town, but as they approached, a woman rushed toward them, crying. "A troop of bandits attacked the town last night," she said. "They charged inside with flaming torches. They burned everything, they robbed everyone, and they took everyone away in chains to sell as slaves. I am the only person who escaped!"

Akiva comforted the woman. Ben Yehudah was too amazed to even speak. Finally he said to Akiva, "Everything I thought was bad turned out to be good. If we had been allowed in the town, the bandits would have captured us. If we had been able to camp by the road, the bandits would have seen us and captured us. If I had been able to stop them as they rode by, they would have captured us and sold us as slaves."

Akiva nodded and said, "You can never know what good will come from anything. That is why I always say, 'Who knows? This, too, can be for the best.' "

NOTES

Rabbi Akiva (c. 50–135 C.E.), the outstanding Torah scholar, began writing down the beliefs, wise sayings, and stories of the great Jewish teachers. His arrangement of the Oral Law according to subjects formed the first part of the Talmud, which was called the *Mishna*.

Akiva also supported Simon Bar Kokhba, who led a revolt against the Romans and the Roman emperor Hadrian from 132 to 135 C.E. Furious, Hadrian passed laws forbidding Jews to study Torah, to observe the Sabbath or any other holy days, and to practice any Jewish traditions. The penalty for being caught was death. Akiva continued to teach Torah openly (under a tree) in defiance of the Roman laws. When asked if he feared the Romans, he answered with the parable of the fox and the fish. In spite of the courage of many, the revolt failed, and as a result, both Bar Kokhba and Akiva were killed by the Romans. Many others were killed, died of starvation, or were taken away as slaves. Judea (as Israel was called at that time) was turned into such a wasteland that the survivors were forced into exile. Israel would not be the home of the Jewish people again for more than eighteen hundred years. It is hard to imagine anything worse.

Yet, Akiva would have said, "This, too, is for the best." The Romans were exhausted by the war and gave up trying to destroy the Jewish identity. Akiva's heroic life and death inspired others to keep their beliefs, and the Jews survived as a people.

There is a Talmudic story (*Ta'anit*) about Nahum, who is called Nahum Gam zu Letova (Nahum This-Too-Is-for-the-Best) because that was his philosophy of life. During the reign of the Roman emperor Caesar, the Jews decided to send the emperor a gift of precious gems. Nahum was chosen to deliver the gift. However, at the inn, the gems were stolen and the chest filled with earth instead. When Nahum was brought before the emperor and the chest was opened, the emperor was furious. Elijah the Prophet suddenly appeared and told the soldiers to toss up some of the magical earth. Instantly, the earth became swords and spears, and with them, the emperor was able to conquer cities. He, in turn, rewarded the Jews. When the thieves heard of this good fortune, they brought chests filled with earth to the emperor, hoping for this same miracle. However, their earth remained earth. The emperor ordered that they be put to death. Nahum continued to say, "This, too, is for the best" for the rest of his days. (See a version of this story, "Miracles All Around," in Peninnah Schram's *Jewish Stories One Generation Tells Another*.)

SOURCES AND VARIANTS

Sources for the tale about Akiva and the bandits are from the Babylonian Talmud, Berakhot 60b; Rashi; and Ta'anit 21A.

The Talmudic tale also appears in Bialik and Ravnitzky's *The Book of Legends*, 236:166.

The parable of the fox and the fish is from the Babylonian Talmud, Berakhot 61b. It is a well-known parable that can be found in many sources, including "The Fox and the Fish" in Jules Harlow's *Lessons from Our Living Past*; "The Parable of the Wise Fishes" in Nathan Ausubel's *A Treasury of Jewish Folklore*.

Motif: J 758:3—Fish refuses fox's invitation to live on dry land and thus escape danger of fisherman)

The Special Ingredient

In the King Solomon story "The Starling's Answer," the bird did not communicate through words; he communicated through actions. Sometimes the truth does not come through words or through actions. Sometimes the truth is tasted, as in this wisdom tale.

THE ROMAN EMPEROR ANTONINUS WAS HUNTING IN THE WOODS when he was caught in a storm and became separated from his companions. He wandered for hours until he was tired and hungry. Finally he saw a house, and he knocked on the door. An old couple answered.

"I am lost," he told them.

"Please join us," they told him. "It's an honor to have a guest!" They made him feel very comfortable.

"It's Friday night, the beginning of our Jewish Sabbath," they said. "We work hard all week, but tonight we celebrate with everything we have." They lit two white candles and recited a blessing over them. They sat in the glow of the candlelight, singing their favorite songs and telling their favorite stories.

At first the emperor thought they were foolish, odd characters, but soon he began to sing as well and share stories long-forgotten. He even laughed for the first time in years.

When it was time for supper, the old couple served hot chicken soup. The emperor said, "This soup tastes wonderful. How did you make it?"

The old man and woman showed him exactly how they prepared and cooked it. The emperor wrote down everything, word for word. He rested all the next day, and then the couple showed him the way out of the woods. As soon as the emperor reached home, he gave the recipe to his cooks, and they prepared the soup. However, it did not taste as good. They tried again. This time he watched to be sure they made no mistake, but the soup tasted quite ordinary.

"Something is missing," he said. "That old couple didn't tell me everything. They left out some special ingredient." It bothered him so much that he traveled back to their home.

"Welcome, good guest," they said.

"I tried to make your soup, but it didn't taste as good. Tell me your special ingredient," asked the emperor.

The couple stared at him in surprise. They turned to each other and spoke quietly, then they nodded and said. "We are happy to tell you what made our soup taste so wonderful to you."

"First," said the woman, "you were tired and troubled."

"Second," said the old man, "you rested and relaxed."

"Third," said the woman, "you enjoyed good company, good stories, and lots of song and laughter."

The emperor felt confused. He said, "What's all that got to do with how the soup tastes?"

"That's what made it taste so good," they said. "The soup was not prepared in a special way for you. You were prepared in a special way for the soup. You felt the happiness that we feel every time we stop working and worrying and we celebrate our day of rest. That's our special ingredient."

The emperor smiled and placed gold coins in their hands. Then he gently placed his arms upon their shoulders. "My good friends," he said. "Let me visit you again and again and share the taste of happiness."

NOTES

The Sabbath marks the seventh day, when we are told that God rested after six days of creation. The Jews celebrate the Sabbath on Saturday. It begins on Friday night at sunset and ends on Saturday night one hour after sunset. Just before the Sabbath begins, the woman of the house lights and recites a blessing over two (or more) white candles. The man of the house then blesses the children and praises his wife by singing "Eshet Chayil" (Woman of Valor).

The Sabbath meal is meant to be the best meal of the week. Traditionally, it is served with wine and two loaves of braided bread called *challah*, over which blessings are first recited. Friends and family talk, sing, and share stories.

Sabbath is a time for rest and joy, a time devoted to study and prayer, a day of spiritual harmony and peace. As Abraham Joshua Heschel writes in his book *The Sabbath: Its Meaning for Modern Man*: "Judaism is a *religion of time* aiming at *the sanctification of time*" (8). No work is to be done, not even turning lights on or off, cooking, traveling, or using the phone, because those actions involve some sort of work.

The Sabbath ends when the first three stars appear in the night sky, twenty-five hours after the onset of the Sabbath. *Havdalah* means separation because that is the act of separation from the Sabbath. At this time of transition from holy to secular time, the four wicks of the Havdalah candle, made of thin candles woven together, are lit. Then the Havdalah blessings are recited over wine, sweet-smelling spices, and the special multiwick (and often multicolored) candle. This ceremony is a mirror image of the one welcoming in the Sabbath. It is traditional to sing "Eliyahu Ha-Navi" (Elijah the Prophet) at the end before wishing one another a good week as the Shabbat ends and the secular time of the weekday routine returns. Havdalah is a ceremony that began over two thousand years ago. The observances of the Sabbath and Havdalah and their meaning are connected to symbolic interpretations and *midrashim*.

COMMENTARY

In one early version, the old man was Rabbi Judah ha-Nasi, the great scholar who collected and organized the Oral Laws into the Mishnah in 200 C.E. Legend has it that he was a good friend of the Emperor Antoninus. This Roman emperor (86–161 C.E.) ruled from 138 to 161 C.E. He repealed his predecessor Hadrian's harsh policies in Judea and allowed Jews to engage freely in their traditional worship. That is why he is featured in many legends in the Talmud and Midrash as engaging in discussions with distinguished rabbis.

In some of the versions of this known tale, the king is in disguise and returns to his palace with the recipe for the delicious soup or meal. Of course, when the royal chef duplicates the recipe, the king is dissatisfied with the food because he soon learns that it lacks the "special ingredient" of Shabbat.

SOURCES AND VARIANTS

The sources are *Shabbat*, 119a and *Midrash*, Genesis *Rabbah*, 11:4.

The two Talmudic sources can be found in Bialik and Ravnitzky's *The Book of Legends*, 491:64 and 492:65. In the first, Caesar asked Rabbi Joshua ben Hananiah: "Why do Sabbath dishes have such a fragrant aroma?" The response was that it is because of the "special seasoning called Sabbath." In the second source, Rabbi Judah I, the Patriarch entertained Antoninus on a Sabbath. The emperor found that even the cold dishes on the Sabbath tasted better than the hot dishes served during the week. When he asked why, the Rabbi replied: "The hot dishes lack Sabbath. Does your pantry have Sabbath?"

"The Missing Ingredient" is in Barbara Diamond Goldin's *The Child's Book of Midrash*.

"The Secret Ingredient" is in Molly Cone's *Stories of Jewish Symbols*.

"The Secret Ingredient" is in Grace Ragues Maisel and Samantha Shubert's *A Year of Jewish Stories*.

A version of *Shabbat*, 119a (between Caesar Hadrian and Rabbi Joshua) appears as "The Joy of Sabbath" in *Saving the World Entire and 100 Other Beloved Parables from the Talmud* by Rabbi Bradley R. Bleefeld and Robert L. Shook.

A version of *Genesis Rabbah*, 11:4 (between Antoninus and Rabbi Judah) appears in "The String of Pearls" section in *Stories from the Rabbis* by Abram S. Isaacs.

A Special Way of Thinking

After the Jewish people were expelled from their homeland, they wandered the world. Since they had no country of their own, their laws, stories, and beliefs became an important way to keep their identity.

Many became scholars who dedicated themselves to studying the Torah and the Talmud. It wasn't enough to be smart. It wasn't enough to have a great amount of knowledge. A scholar also needed to know how to discuss, debate, and develop ideas. A scholar needed a special way of thinking. This story is an imaginative and clever way of explaining that special way of thinking.

A YOUNG MAN FOUND A SCHOLAR WHO WAS A MASTER OF THE TALMUD. The young man asked, "Will you teach me the Talmud?"

The scholar answered, "It won't do you any good."

"Why not?" asked the young man.

The scholar said, "First you need to know the Talmud's way of thinking."

"Fine!" said the young man. "Then teach me the Talmud's way of thinking."

"That won't do you any good, either," said the scholar. "Not unless you have the ability to learn the Talmud's way of thinking."

"How will I know if I have the ability?" asked the young man.

The scholar said, "I will test you with three questions."

"Fine," said the young man. "What's the first question?"

The scholar said, "Two men climb down a filthy soot-filled chimney. One comes out with a dirty face, one with a clean face. Who decides to wash his face?"

The young man answered, "The one with the dirty face."

"No," said the scholar. "It's the one with the clean face. Let me explain. The one with the dirty face sees his friend's clean face. He assumes his own face must also be clean. So he decides not to wash. The one with the clean face sees his friend's dirty face, and he thinks,

'My face must also be dirty.' So naturally he washes."

The young man looked embarrassed. "I didn't think about it that way. What's the second question?"

"Two men climb down a filthy soot-filled chimney. One comes out with a dirty face, one with a clean face. Who decides to wash his face?"

The young man laughed and said, "I already know the answer. It's the one with the clean face."

"No," said the scholar, "it's the one with the dirty face. Let me explain. The one with the dirty face sees his friend's clean face. He says to his friend, 'Your face is so clean! Is my face also that clean?' His friend answers, 'No, your face is filthy.' So naturally he washes."

The young man looked upset. "I thought the first answer was the right one."

The scholar said, "The first answer was right until you think of the second answer. The second answer is such a better answer that the first answer is no longer acceptable."

"I see your point," said the young man. "What's the third question?"

"Two men climb down a filthy soot-filled chimney. One comes out with a dirty face, one with a clean face. Who decides to wash his face?"

The young man frowned, "You won't get me this time," he said. "It won't be the one with the dirty face, and it won't be the one with the clean face. The answer has to be either both of them or neither of them."

"No," said the scholar. "There is no answer because the question is ridiculous. How can two men climb down a filthy soot-filled chimney and one come out clean and one come out dirty? It's not reasonable."

The young man looked shocked. "I was wrong all three times. I must be the wrong person to learn the Talmud."

"No," said the scholar. "You are the right person to learn the Talmud. Let me explain. If you could answer everything correctly, why would you need me to teach you? You will be an excellent student. Look how much you have already learned about the Talmud's way of thinking!"

The scholar accepted the young man, and he became an excellent student of the Talmud.

NOTES

Non-Jews refer to the first five books of the Hebrew Bible as the Old Testament. The Hebrew Bible is actually made up of the Torah (the Five Books of Moses), the Prophets, and the Writings.

The Talmud comes later. It is a huge collection of laws, debates, stories, wise sayings, and commentaries that fills sixty-three large books. It covers one thousand years of learning, from about 500 B.C.E to 500 C.E.

COMMENTARY

As the Torah (the five books of the Hebrew Bible) is written in shorthand, the Talmud (the commentaries on the Torah) is written in a cryptic style including, even intertwining, *Halakha* (normative law and codes of behavior) and *Agada* (stories, legends, parables, animal tales, allegories, and so on, which contain the spirit of the oral law). The Talmud, which means "study" or "learning" in Hebrew, was transmitted from generation to generation in the oral tradition before it was finally codified and written down.

"By the early second century C.E., Rabbi Akiva is credited as the first person to codify rabbinic teaching. By the turn of the third century C.E., Rabbi Yehuda HaNasi completed editing and collecting all the written and unwritten portions from the various schools, countries, and rabbinic authorities. These teachings comprised the *Mishna*. Over succeeding generations, groups of rabbis gathered to study these sacred texts, the Torah and the Mishna, and to teach them orally, in the same manner as in the years before. These interpreters and Jewish scholars, known as *Amoraim* (Aramaic for 'spokesmen'), communicated lessons of the rabbis to the students, especially in the land of Israel and Babylonia in the third to sixth centuries after the conclusion of the Mishna. From their clarifications of passages and disputes over other meanings and interpretations, there evolved a second text, the *Gemara* (Aramaic for 'study'). Together, the Mishna and Gemara make up the "Talmud" (from Peninnah Schram's essay, "Jewish Models: Adapting Folktales for Telling Aloud" in *Who Says? Essays on Pivotal Issues in Contemporary Storytelling*, edited by Carol L. Birch and Melissa A. Heckler (67).

Since the Talmud records oral discussions and interpretations, even of later Jewish scholars, there is no easy systematic arrangement of the subjects. It is, however, a great, treasured, sacred storehouse of Jewish law and lore that has had unparalleled influence on Jewish thought, practice, and study.

Torah can also mean the entire body of Jewish teaching and sacred literature.

For further study of the Talmud, see Adin Steinsaltz's English translation, *The Talmud,* with his summary and commentary, published by Random House. These multivolumed texts allow the nonscholar to be able to swim in the "Sea of Talmud."

SOURCES AND VARIANTS

This story of Talmudic reasoning is a well-known tale, and most likely originated as a folkloristic anecdote. It can be found as "A Lesson in Talmud" in Nathan Ausubel's *A Treasury of Jewish Folklore.*

An illustrative story for the category of "Talmud" is in Leo Rosten's *The New Joys of Yiddish.* Lawrence Bush adds an interesting commentary in this new edition of this valuable resource by commenting on Rosten's use of Goebbels, the Nazi minister of propaganda, who approaches an elderly rabbi to ask: "Jew! I have heard that you Jews employ a special form of reasoning called Talmudic, which explains your cleverness. I want you to teach it to me." The historical note explains that before the printing press, during the medieval period, the Catholic Church would often burn the Talmud, hoping that the Jewish community, deprived of its sacred texts, would become more vulnerable to conversion. "Usually the burning would be preceded by a 'disputation,' in which Jewish sages would be forced into debating theology with church officials and vainly defending the Jewish community from anti-Semitic slanders. Because of the wide-ranging, uncensored nature of Talmudic discussion, these slanders might often be rooted in passages of the Talmud itself" (391–392).

An unsourced version of this story appears in Henry D. Spalding's *Encyclopedia of Jewish Humor: From Biblical Times to the Modern Age,* and in an orally transmitted version as "What Is Talmud?" in Nina Jaffe and Steve Zeitlin's *While Standing on One Foot.*

A version also appears in David Novak and Moshe Waldok's *The Big Book of Jewish Humor.*

Another version of this story is found in the chapter "Two Men Come Down a Chimney: Jewish Intelligence and the Playful Logic of the Jewish Mind" in Rabbi Joseph Telushkin's *Jewish Humor: What the Best Jewish Jokes Say About the Jew,* based on the article "The Logic of the Talmud" by Sol Jacobson in *Midstream,* Vol. XXII, No. 6, June/July 1976, page 50.

The Magic Seed

When the Jews lost their homeland, they were scattered across the Roman Empire, which surrounded the Mediterranean Sea. Some went to Europe to the north, while others lived in the Arab lands to the south.

   During the Golden Age in Spain, as well as in Morocco and other Middle Eastern countries, Jews and Arabs shared a love of mathematics, medicine, literature, and philosophy. However, the rulers, who were called sultans, could be unpredictable and dangerous to both Jew and Arab alike. There are many tales in which someone's survival required fast thinking and good luck. In this story from the Jews of Morocco, a victim saves himself by testing his accusers.

A HUNGRY BEGGAR WAS CAUGHT STEALING A LOAF OF BREAD. THE sultan said, "You will pay for that bread with your head. Your death will teach others not to steal."

The sultan's guards dragged the poor beggar into the open courtyard. The executioner raised a huge curved sword. Just before the blade came down, the beggar called out, "Kill me if you want, but do not throw away my magic seed."

"Stop the execution," said the sultan. "Tell me, beggar, what kind of magic power does your seed possess?"

The beggar answered, "It will grow instantly into a tree of ripe pomegranates. Who wants it?"

Everyone wanted it. The beggar offered it to the sultan's head minister, the vizier, and said, "Plant it right here and now in the courtyard. But be warned; this seed will only grow if you have never stolen anything." The vizier turned pale and confessed, "Your seed will not grow for me. Once when I was a child, I took a valuable toy from my friend, and I never gave it back."

"Perhaps the sultan's general wants the seed," said the beggar. But the sultan's general shook his head, saying, "It will not grow for me. Once, the sultan sent me a message that I must come to him at once. I was in such a rush that I took another man's horse, and I never bothered to give it back."

The beggar then turned to the sultan, saying, "Will you plant this magic seed, O sultan?"

The sultan lowered his eyes and answered, "It will not grow for me, either. Once I argued with another sultan, and we fought each other in a war. I won and took his entire country from him."

The beggar said, "I never took a country or a horse or even a toy. I only took a loaf of bread because I was starving."

The sultan smiled and said, "I do not know if your seed is truly magic, but I do know that you are truly clever. How can I punish you when I have acted so much worse?" The sultan set the beggar free and gave him a job as a royal gardener.

NOTES

Europe became Christian, and later the Arab lands became Muslim. The Jews were not only seen as outsiders, but also as outsiders who had a different religion.

This tale was told by both Jews and Arabs, and the beggar is not necessarily Jewish. Jews would have found the tale meaningful because they sometimes felt that their situation was as difficult as the beggar's.

COMMENTARY

In 1492, King Ferdinand and Queen Isabella expelled all the Jews from Spain. These *Sephardim* went to many countries in the Middle East, as well as Morocco, Turkey, Italy, Greece, Yugoslavia, Holland, and England. Jews had also come to Morocco at earlier periods, possibly as early as the First Temple. However, documented records show Jews living in Morocco from the second century B.C.E. The fate of the Jews varied according to the ruler. In Morocco, Jews lived, for the most part, in a walled Jewish quarter called the *mellah*, under the protection of the king. Because of this, the mellah was very different from the East European ghetto.

Nevertheless, the power of life and death over everyone was held by the ruler. Throughout the centuries, when Jews had no religious, economic, or political power, they had to live by their wits and resourceful thinking. A story that offers clever word defenses and a creative approach in teaching perspective to someone in a powerful position becomes a folktale. After all, what is a folktale but a story transmitted by generations, one that contains the seeds of wisdom needed by the folk, that is, the common people. This story reinforces the idea that out of desperation, quick wit, and a seemingly worthless seed comes a valuable lesson to us all.

SOURCES AND VARIANTS

The story is in Moses Gaster's *The Exempla of the Rabbis*. A version of this story appears in Nathan Ausubel's *A Treasury of Jewish Folklore* as "The Wise Rogue," under the category of "Rogues and Sinners." It is also published as "The Seeds of Honesty" in *A Year of Jewish Stories*, by Grace Ragues Maisel and Samantha Shubert, and as "The Clever Thief" in Barbara Diamond Goldin's *A Child's Book of Midrash*.

An unsourced variant is "The Magic Seed" in *Jewish Folktales*, by Leo Pavlat.

There are two variants in the Israel Folktale Archives:

IFA 8230 from Morocco, told by Aliza Anidjar (Tanger) and recorded by Yfrah Haviv. This version is published in *The Treasure of Our Fathers*, edited by Tamar Alexander and Dov Noy. IFA 22463 from Iraqi Kurdistan (Zako), recorded by Yehuda Atzaba in 2002.

Tale Types: AT 929—Clever defenses
AT 1526—Escapes from arrest by trickery
Motifs: H 501.5*—Test of wisdom
J 1110—Clever persons
K 500—Escapes from arrest by trickery

The True Jewel of Their Father

Medieval Spain was a land of great learning and freedom, where Christians, Muslims, and Jews lived and worked as equals.

It was called the Golden Age because it was a time of peace and opportunity, which Jews would not see again until modern times. However, it was not perfect. Sometimes there were problems that had to be faced with courage and with wisdom, as we see in this story.

SALADIN, THE SULTAN WHO RULED THE MUSLIMS OF SPAIN, HAD been arguing with Don Pedro of Aragon, the king of the Christians of Spain. Each claimed that his religion was the true one. They called a Jewish leader and scholar named Ephraim Santzi to decide who was right. They said, "Tell us, who has God's true religion? The Christians, Muslims, or the Jews?"

Ephraim did not want to insult Christians or Muslims. He also did not want to bring shame on his own people. He asked for three days to decide. When he returned he told this story.

"There was a large and precious ruby that had a wonderful power. Whoever held it close to his heart found that his life was blessed with kindness and understanding. It was owned by a jeweler who cut and polished it so perfectly that everyone was astonished by its beauty.

The jeweler had three grown sons. Each one wanted the ruby more than anything else. The time came for the jeweler to go on a long journey. Each son begged him for the jewel.

As he was about to leave, the jeweler met with each son separately. He gave each one a ruby, saying, "This is for you and for you alone." When he was gone, the three sons were surprised to see that the three rubies looked identical. They said, "Our father must have owned two other rubies. He has cut and polished them to look exactly like the true one."

Each son claimed that he had the true jewel and that the other jewels were false. They argued and accused each other of lies and trickery. Finally, they went to a judge and told him the whole story. They then asked him, "Which is the true jewel?"

The judge studied all three rubies, but he could not see a single important difference. Finally, he said, "I cannot tell you. Only your father knows the answer." The sons were deeply distressed. They were about to leave when the judge spoke again. "I can tell you how to prove that your jewel is not a false one."

"Tell us!" they begged.

He told them, "Whoever holds the true jewel close to his heart finds that his life is blessed with kindness and understanding. Live your life in such a way that you always act with kindness and understanding. Then the whole world will say that your jewel cannot be false because your life is truly blessed."

Saladin and Don Pedro smiled at each other. Saladin said, "Thank you, Ephraim. I understand why you have told us this story."

"I also understand," said Don Pedro. "Each of us—Christian, Muslim, and Jew—must make himself worthy of the gift his Father gave him."

NOTES

During the Golden Age of Spain, Jews could discuss their beliefs freely. Later, in Spain and other lands, it became dangerous. Jews sometimes had to defend their religion in a public debate. If the Jewish scholar won, he might be punished. If he lost, it could lead to demands that Jews give up their religion and convert.

In the original version of the story, King Don Pedro of Aragon is asked by the troubadour Nicholas of Valencia to have Ephraim Sancho (or Santzi) (980–1060) tell which is the true religion, Jewish or Christian. Ephraim Sancho requested three days to consider his decision. When he came before the king, he told the king of a father, a jeweler, who gave jewels to each of his two sons. Ephraim was asked to judge which jewel was more valuable. Since he could not tell one jewel from the other, he told the sons to ask their father, and they beat him. The two sons were Esau and Jacob. Ephraim then told them that only the jeweler, God, could know the true value of the jewels.

COMMENTARY

Asking a Jew to judge between religions is a no-win situation. However, answering a question with a story is very much a Jewish tradition. This type of story-within-a-story can be found not only in folktales, but also in the Torah as a way to teach in a nonthreatening way. For example, God sent Nathan the Prophet to rebuke King David for intentionally sending Bathsheba's husband to the front line of battle, where he would assuredly be killed. David would then be able to marry Bathsheba. How did Nathan rebuke the king? He told King David a parable about a shepherd (II Samuel, Chapter 12). Only when David heard the parable paralleling his actions did he understand the repercussions of his actions and take responsibility for what he had done. Stories illuminate and teach in a beautiful and lasting way.

The *Dubner Maggid*, for one, always used the opportunity to teach a lesson by saying: "Give me a moment and let me tell you a story." In this way, the arrow always hit its mark.

The story of the jewels also reminds me of a story I heard years ago about a report that the Messiah was going to visit a certain town. But since no one knew who he would be or how they would recognize him, each person began to act toward his or her neighbor as though that person might be the Messiah. And everyone became kindly, generous, courteous, and hospitable. The town became transformed into a welcoming and gracious community.

SOURCES AND VARIANTS

Shevet Yehudah, by Shelomoh ben Verga, Ed. M. Wiener.

In Micha Joseph Bin Gorion's *Der Born Judas*, V.

Also in Haim Schwarzbaum's *Studies in Jewish and World Folklore*.

"The Two Gems" is in *The Folklore of the Jews*, by Angelo S. Rappoport.

"The Parable of the Two Precious Stones" is in Micha Joseph Bin Gorion's *Mimekor Yisrael*, Volume 1.

"The Magic Ring" is in *101 Jewish Stories*, collected by Simon Certner.

The Worst Poison

Moses Ben Maimon also had to face a dangerous test created by a powerful sultan. It was not only a test of his intelligence and skill, it was also a test of his beliefs. Maimon believed, as a doctor and as a Jew, that he should not kill anyone. But what if someone were trying to kill him?

WHEN MAIMON ARRIVED IN EGYPT, HE WAS CALLED TO THE PALACE of Sultan Al Fadil. He found the grand court filled with the best doctors in the land. The sultan entered and announced, "I have called you all here because I want a new doctor. Whoever I choose will gain great wealth and power."

Maimon did not care for either wealth or power, but he thought, "If I become the sultan's doctor, I will be able to help myself and help my people."

The sultan tested all the doctors with difficult questions until there were only two left, Maimon and Kammun. Kammun said, "Great Sultan, I am a better doctor than Maimon. I can cure the blind."

"No one can do that," said Maimon.

Kammun laughed scornfully and called for a man, who stumbled into the room with blank eyes. Kammun covered the man's eyes with a secret ointment. He mumbled strange words, then he washed the ointment off. The man blinked and stared at everything as if amazed.

"Behold!" said Kammun. "I have cured the blind!"

Maimon suspected trickery. "How long were you blind?" he asked the man.

"Since birth," said the man.

"What do I hold in my hand?" asked Maimon.

"A scarf," said the man.

"What color is it?" asked Maimon

"It is red," said the man.

"You are correct," said Maimon. "But you have not revealed the truth," Maimon explained. "This man claims that he was blind since birth. If that were true, he would not know the names of any colors. He could not say that the scarf is red."

"You are right, Maimon," said the sultan. "The man was not blind."

Kammun fell upon his knees before the sultan, "I was not trying to trick you. The man lied to me as well. Give me another chance."

"Why should I?" asked the sultan.

Kammun smiled slyly. "You have many enemies. You need protection from assassins, especially from poisoners," said Kammun. "I know more than Maimon knows about poisons and their antidotes."

"Prove it!" said the sultan.

Kammun said, "Let Maimon and me poison each other. The one who survives is the winner."

"I am a doctor, not a killer," said Maimon. "I will defend myself, but I will not take a life, not even Kammun's."

The sultan raised his hand for silence. He announced, "The two of you shall remain in the palace. You shall sleep in the same room and eat at the same table. Use whatever poisons you wish. The one who survives is the winner."

Day after day, Maimon and Kammun watched each other very carefully, never knowing when the other might slip something deadly into his food or drink, or onto a pillow or a brush. Kammun found many ways to poison Maimon. He put a drop of a certain poison on Maimon's shirt so it would penetrate his skin, he scattered poisonous dust on Maimon's pillow so that he would breathe it in while he slept. However, Maimon identified every poison and always found an antidote.

Kammun was amazed that Maimon survived all his powerful poisons. He began to worry about what poisons Maimon was using against him. Day after day, his fear increased. Kammun avoided food and drink; he hardly slept or changed his clothes. He would not touch anything or even breathe deeply. Finally, he had to drink something. He saw Maimon pouring himself a glass of milk. He thought, "His drink must be safe," so he grabbed it out of Maimon's hand and gulped it down.

"Ah," said Maimon with a knowing look, "I knew the time would come. You had to drink something."

Kammun turned deathly pale. He screamed, "You've tricked me. You wanted me to drink that milk. It's poisoned!" Kammun felt his throat tighten. His hands trembled and he grew dizzy. He rushed out, desperately trying to guess the kind of poison he had swallowed. He could not detect any unusual taste or smell. He tried every antidote he knew, risking more and more dangerous cures. In the morning the guards found Kammun lying cold and still on the white marble floor of the courtyard.

The sultan called for Maimon. Maimon examined Kammun and announced, "O Sultan, his heart has stopped."

"You shall be my doctor," said the Sultan. "But tell me, what poison did you use to kill Kammun?"

"I did not use any poison," said Maimon. "I am a doctor. I save lives; I do not take them."

"If there was no poison in the milk, then how did Kammun die?" the sultan asked.

"He tortured himself with worry. He made himself sick with dangerous cures. The stress was too much, and his heart collapsed," said Maimon.

"Are you telling me that Kammun killed himself?" the Sultan asked.

Maimon answered, "Kammun's fear destroyed him. Fear is the worst poison of all."

NOTES

Moses Ben Maimon (1135–1204) was also known as Maimonides. He was the most brilliant Jewish scholar of the Middle Ages. He was a genius who wrote important books on law, philosophy, religion, astronomy, and medicine. In addition, he was a leader of his community, and dedicated his life to helping people in need.

Maimon lived in Cordova, Spain, until it was overrun by an army of radical Muslims. He wandered through safer parts of the Arab world until he reached Egypt. The sultan of Egypt, Al Fadil, made him his doctor and advisor. Some historians say that Richard the Lionhearted asked Maimon to be his doctor on his crusade to capture Jerusalem. Others say he became the doctor and advisor of the great Saladin, who ruled the entire Arab world. Saladin appears in the next story.

Arab rulers at that time were often in danger of assassination. Most would not even eat anything until a servant tasted it to check for poison. Some poisons were powerful enough to kill by just touching the skin or by being breathed in.

COMMENTARY

Years ago, when I recorded books for the Jewish Braille Institute, I discovered that, in fact, the only thing a blind person cannot learn is to identify colors. In other words, colors must be seen in order to be known. In this story, Maimonides found a clever way to really know whether the man's sight had been miraculously restored or whether Maimonides would be duped.

Maimonides was also known by the acronym RAMBAM (Rabbi Moses Ben Maimon). In his *Golden Ladder of Charity*, he clarified the eight steps of *tzedakah* (giving of charity/justice), with the highest step being a gift from the heart to help another person earn a livelihood for himself. (In other words, rather than give fish to the hungry, teach them how to fish.)

A story that captured my imagination was about the time Maimonides was called to operate on a man's brain. When he saw that there was a worm on the brain, he realized that to cut out the worm in such a delicate place could be fatal to the patient. What did he do? He took a leaf and placed it near the worm. The worm crawled onto the leaf and, in that clever way, Maimonides saved the man.

SOURCES AND VARIANTS

"Rabbi Moses ben Maimon and the Physicians—The Poison" in Micha Joseph Bin Gorion's *Mimekor Yisrael*.

In Moses Gaster's *Sefer ha-Ma'assiyot* (The Exempla of the Rabbis).

In *Shalshelet ha-Kabbalah*, 33, by Gedaliyah ibn Yahiya.

In Micha Joseph Bin Gorion's *Der Born Judas V*.

In Haim Schwarzbaum's *Studies in Jewish and World Folklore*.

Tale Type: AT 922A - Achikar (only the poison tale)—Falsely accused minister reinstates himself by his cleverness

Motif: K 2101—Falsely accused minister reinstates himself by his cleverness.

The Inquisitor's Test

In this next story, Adam has a contest of wits with a leader of the Spanish Inquisition. The Grand Inquisitor was as ruthless as Kammun and even more deceitful.

THE GRAND INQUISITOR FALSELY ACCUSED A JEWISH SCHOLAR named Adam of terrible crimes. The Grand Inquisitor wanted to appear fair in front of the judges, so he offered Adam a chance to escape execution. He said that he would offer Adam two pieces of paper, one that read INNOCENT, the other that read GUILTY. The paper that Adam chose would decide his fate. However, the Inquisitor had secretly written GUILTY on both papers.

Adam guessed the trick. He snatched one of the papers from the Inquisitioner's hand and swallowed it.

"Why did you do that?" asked the Grand Inquisitor.

"Show us the other piece of paper," said Adam. "If it says GUILTY, then I must have chosen the one that said INNOCENT."

The Grand Inquisitor had to show the other paper, which read GUILTY. He was forced to set Adam free.

NOTES

Spain was a great country, where Jews, Muslims and Christians lived in harmony for centuries. It was called "The Golden Age," which was approximately between the eighth and the thirteenth centuries. It did not last. A radical group of Muslims took over Southern Spain and persecuted both Jews and Christians. Later, Christians took over all of Spain. They began a persecution called the Inquisition and eventually expelled all Muslims and Jews. The Jews were expelled from Spain in 1492, the same year Christopher Columbus discovered America. A few years later, Portugal also expelled its Jews. The Portuguese expelled the adults but forced the children to stay and become Christians.

Some Jews and Muslims pretended to convert to Christianity in order to avoid being expelled, especially without their children. The Inquisition was constantly trying to uncover these false converts. The punishment was being burned at the stake.

COMMENTARY

Even when times were treacherous for the Jews, laughter allowed them to keep their balance. Through stories, Jews could be victorious, besting the anti-Semitic enemy who sought to destroy them. Without control over their physical fate in terrible times, the Jews found they had control through words. This story shows a cleverness of logical thought, as though the Jew said, "Elementary, my dear Watson," when he concluded that he must have swallowed the Innocent sign since the other one read Guilty.

SOURCES AND VARIANTS

Versions can be found in Nathan Ausubel's *A Treasury of Jewish Folklore* and Leo Rosten's *The New Joys of Yiddish*.

Under the category of "Rabbis," this medieval folktale appears in Joseph Telushkin's *Jewish Humor*.

In the Rosten book, the story is used to illustrate the Yiddish word *epes*, which literally means "something" but has many other meanings, depending on the context in which it is used. At the end of the story, the comment is "That was *epes* brilliant!" (95) meaning, in my interpretation, "That was, wow, unbelievably brilliant!"

Tale Types: AT 920-929—Clever acts and words
AT 1526—Escapes from arrest by trickery
Motifs: H 220—Ordeals; guilt or innocence thus established (tests of truth)
H 507—Wit combat; test in repartee

The Wisdom of a Bird

In an earlier story about a starling, Solomon realized how clever a bird could be. We aren't as wise as Solomon, but, hopefully, we aren't as foolish as the hunter in this medieval fable.

ONE DAY A BIRD WAS FLYING FREE AND HAPPY, SAILING UP AND down, swooping between the trees, when suddenly she was caught, trapped in a net, and pulled down to earth into the hands of a hunter.

The hunter gripped her and was about to wring her neck when she cried out, "Hoo, hoo, hoo! Why do want to hurt me! Do you not like me?"

"I like all birds," said the hunter. "I like to catch them and eat them."

"If you set me free," said the bird, "I will give you three."

"Three what?" asked the hunter. "Three wishes?"

"You foolish human," said the bird. "Wishes are no good without wisdom. I will give you three pieces of wisdom."

The hunter scoffed, "What kind of wisdom comes from a bird brain? Ha!"

"Set me free," said the bird, "and my bird wisdom will set you free from pain and trouble."

"Very well," said the hunter. "Give me three pieces of wisdom."

"First," said the bird. "Don't believe anything that has never been done. Second, don't regret anything that is over and done. Third, don't try to do anything that cannot be done."

The hunter repeated what the bird said, "Don't believe anything that has never been done. Don't regret anything that is over and done. Don't try to do anything that cannot be done."

He freed the bird as he had agreed. The bird flew to a branch of a nearby tree, laughing all the way. "Hoo, hoo, hoo! You foolish human. Why did you let me go? If you had eaten me, you would have found my stomach full of diamonds."

"Oh no!" the hunter shouted. "I could have been rich! Come back here!" He began to climb the tree, trying to catch her, but just as he reached her branch, she flew up to a higher one. Branch by branch they went, higher and higher to the very top. There the bird fluttered in the air just out of reach. The hunter grabbed at her but missed and fell, breaking through every branch. *Crack! Smash! Wham!* He landed with an awful thud and lay groaning on the ground.

"Hoo, hoo, hoo!" cooed the bird as she circled overhead. "You foolish human. You forgot everything I taught you! First, I said, 'Don't believe anything that has never been done.' Instead you believed that my stomach was full of diamonds. Hoo, hoo! Birds eat seeds and insects, not diamonds. Second I said, 'Don't regret anything that is over and done.' Instead, you regretted letting me go. Third, I said, 'Don't try to do anything that cannot be done.' Instead you climbed a tree trying to catch a bird. Now look at all your pain and trouble. What good would diamonds do you? No good at all when you don't have the wisdom of a bird."

Off she flew, free and happy as a bird.

NOTES

Fables were invented in Greece or India and became popular among the Romans around 50 C.E. The Jews were living in all parts of the Roman Empire by then, and learned fables from the Romans. But Jews retold the fables in their own versions. They would have brought many fables with them as they found new homes in northern Europe.

Fables have animals, birds, even plants, speaking and acting as if they were humans. Each creature has a recognizable character. Birds, for example, are commonly seen as free and easy-going creatures. People thought they must have pure and wise souls because they could fly so close to Heaven.

COMMENTARY

Fables are wonderful teaching tales because they are short and simple but with a clear moral. In earlier Jewish fables, many of them translated and adapted from Indian, Roman, and Greek sources, the animals were not only endowed with human personalities, but also spoke wisely about Torah. (For more on Jewish fabulists, see Peninnah Schram's *Jewish Stories One Generation Tells Another*, 74–75 and 246–247.)

This tale is known all over Europe and Asia. The Greek verse version by Babrius tells the same story, with a wolf and a fox instead of a man and a bird. The version with the bird, usually a nightingale and often called Philomela, was first known in Europe in the collection of Odo of Cheriton, then found its way into the canon of Aesop. It also appears in *The Arabian Nights*.

Sometimes, the bird is a nightingale or a quail or just "a wise bird." Its treasure is a jewel or pearl as big as an ostrich egg, an eagle egg, or a goose egg. In Jewish lore, the bird knows the seventy languages of mankind, a common Jewish motif.

In the version "Three Precepts" (See Sources below), at the end of the story the bird quotes Proverbs to the hunter: "'A reproof entereth more into a wise man than an hundred stripes into a fool' " (Proverbs XVII,10).

SOURCES
Earliest source is the collection of Odo of Cheriton (twelfth century).

An early Jewish version is "Haggadot Ketu'ot;" in *Ha-Goren IX*, edited by S.A. Horodezky; and in *Ben ha-Melekh ve-ha-Nazir*; in Micha Joseph Bin Gorion's *Der Born Judas*; in Moses Gaster's *The Exempla of the Rabbis*; and in Chaim Schwarzbaum's *Studies in Jewish and World Folklore*.

Two versions of "The Huntsman and the Bird" can also be found in Bin Gorion's *Mimekor Yisrael*.

"The Wise Bird and the Foolish Man" is in Nathan Ausubel's *A Treasury of Jewish Folklore*.

"The Bird's Wisdom" is in Peninnah Schram's *Jewish Stories One Generation Tells Another*.

"The Hunter and the Bird" is in Simon Certner's *101 Jewish Stories*.

"The Three Counsels of the Cock" (IFA 7663) was collected by Zvi Haimovitz from Yerahmiel Feler (Poland) in Edna Cheichel's *A Tale for Each Month 1967*.

"Three Precepts" is in *The Folklore of the Jews*, by Angelo S. Rappoport.

Tale Types: AT 150—Advice of the fox (bird)
AT 910—Precepts bought or given prove correct.
Motifs: B 122.1—Advice from bird
J 21.12—Rue not a thing that is past.
J 21.13—Never believe that which is beyond belief.
J 21.14—Never try to reach the unattainable.
K 604—Man releases bird if the latter will give him three counsels.

The Wound That Did Not Heal

As we grow up, we hear many children's rhymes, such as "Sticks and stones will break my bones, but words will never hurt me." This story shows how just the opposite is true. In Judaism we know that words are important and powerful. Words can have a lasting effect for positive or negative results.

A MAN WENT TO THE WILDERNESS TO KILL A LION. HE HAD defeated all other beasts, but he feared the lion because it was so powerful and fast. The lion could smell him and hear him from far away. It could creep behind him as silently as a shadow.

When the lion saw the hunter approaching, it was also afraid. The lion had defeated all other beasts, but it feared the hunter because he was so clever and skillful. The hunter's arrows were like flying teeth. His knife was longer and sharper than the lion's claws.

The lion called to the hunter, "Why do you want to kill me?"

The hunter answered, "Because you are so dangerous."

The lion said, "You are also dangerous. We fear each other. That makes us hate each other, and that makes us want to kill each other. Let's make peace instead. Then we will not fear or hate or hurt each other."

The hunter was glad to make peace. He and the lion became friends. They met every day. They hunted together and shared everything they caught. They also shared everything they knew. The man taught the lion about human beings, and the lion taught the man about animals.

"I am glad we made peace," the hunter said. "It is better than having to hurt you in a fight."

"Yes," said the lion. "It would have been terrible if I had killed and eaten you. I would not have known you as a friend."

The hunter laughed and answered, "You would not have killed me. If we had fought, I would have won."

"My good friend," said the lion. "I am the king of all the animals. My roar is like thunder that shakes the earth and terrifies all living things. My paws can smash young trees with a single blow. No creature can survive if I attack."

The man frowned and told the lion, "You were created to rule the other animals, but humans were created to rule the world and everything upon it. Therefore, I am more powerful than you."

They continued to disagree until they came to the ruins of an ancient palace. They stared at the collapsed pillars and the broken roof. Then the man noticed a picture carved on a large block of stone. "Look at that. It proves that humans are better than lions."

The stone carving showed a king sitting on a throne. A lion was crouched at his feet, bowing down to him.

The lion looked carefully. It smelled the stone and poked it with its paw. It said, "That is not a real lion, and that is not a real man. They are only images carved in the stone. Who made that thing?"

The hunter answered, "A human carved it."

The lion snorted. "Then it means nothing. If I could carve, I would make a picture of a human bowing down to a lion."

The man became angry. He kicked dirt at the lion's feet and yelled, "You don't understand anything! You are just a stupid animal. You don't deserve to be my friend." He turned his back on the lion and walked home.

The next day, the man went out to meet the lion and greeted him as if nothing had happened. The lion did not answer. For a while they walked together in silence. Finally the lion stopped beside a heavy stick and told the man, "Pick up that stick and hit me on the head with all your strength."

The man turned pale and backed away. He said, "We promised to keep peace between us. We promised to stay friends. I cannot hurt you."

The lion snarled. He growled and then he roared, "By the peace that we have made and by the friendship we have shared, I demand you strike me!"

The man did not know how to refuse. He picked up the heavy stick and struck the lion on the head so hard that the lion fell down on the ground and was soaked in blood. The man dropped the stick and ran away, horrified by what he had done.

The man did not return for many weeks, but finally he searched for the lion and found him. "My friend," he said. "Are you still in pain from what I did to you?"

The lion gazed at the man quietly for a time, then said, "I am in pain, and I am not in pain from what you did to me. Look at the wound you made with your stick."

The man examined the wound and saw that it had healed completely. "Has it stopped hurting?" he asked.

"This wound no longer hurts me," said the lion, "but my other wound still hurts."

"What wound is that?" the hunter asked.

"The wound you gave when you insulted me with cruel and angry words."

The man remembered what he had said to the lion in front of the stone carving. "But they were only words," he said. "How can they hurt such a powerful creature as you."

The lion shook his head and said, "It makes no difference whether I am an animal or a human being, the hurt caused by cruel words can be more painful than any wound caused by a stick." Saying this, the lion left him.

Some say the lion died from sadness.

Some say it was the man who became sick and died from shame. Others say the man discovered the way to cure the lion's suffering and his own shame; he offered a deeply felt apology. He told the lion that he was wrong, that he was sorry he caused such pain, and that he would never speak such hurtful words again. They say that the lion and the man became wiser and better friends than they had ever been before.

NOTES

The first part of the story is based on a tale, "The Lion and the Hunter," from *The Fox Fables of Berechiah ha-Nakdan*, twelfth-century France. The second section, which begins with the insult, is based on a Kurdistani folktale found in *The Folk Literature of the Kurdistani Jews: An Anthology* from Iraqi Kurdistan. In that tale, a hunter befriends a serpent, and the hunter's wife insults the creature when the man brings it home as his guest.

The lion was once common across the Middle East as a symbol of strength and majesty. As a result of these qualities, the lion became a symbol of ancient Jerusalem and modern Israel. Its image can often be seen on the mantle and silver breastplate covering the Torah, and it is often shown guarding the base of the Hanukkah lamp, called a Hanukkiah.

The end of this story illustrates the concept of forgiveness that developed later in the medieval period. Maimonides had written extensively on repentance and forgiveness. In chapter 2, halachah 2, of Hilchos Teshuva (The Laws of Repentance), Maimonides (known also as the Rambam) said that one must take several steps in order to gain "complete *teshuva*" or repentance. The four steps are: 1) you must leave the sin, 2) you must regret the sin, 3) God must testify that you will never do the sin again, and 4) you must confess the sin verbally.

COMMENTARY

Animal fables teach values by illustrating an important moral or ethical lesson. As cautionary tales, the moral is usually printed at the end of the fable. However, in *Fables of a Jewish Aesop*, Moses Hadas's translation of *The Fox Fables of Berchiah ha-Nakdan*, a stated moral is at the beginning of the tale. For the fable upon which "The Wound That Did Not Heal" is based, the moral is "Many are the workers of iniquity and the speakers of destruction, for hearts are not equable."

In Judaism, words are synonymous with action. Therefore, words are treated with great respect, and even an alphabet letter or part of a letter can be powerful and can have a world-shattering effect in its interpretation.

Two of the most effecting lines in Jewish text are "Who is the man that desireth life, loveth days, that he may see good therein? Keep thy tongue from evil, and thy lips from speaking guile" (Psalm 34:13-14); and "I said, I will take heed to my ways, that I sin not with my tongue; I will keep a curb upon my mouth, while the wicked is before me" (Psalm 39:2). Words (or the tongue) can be used for good or for evil.

Two stories come to mind that illustrate the importance of using words carefully. The first one is about a woman who spreads gossip harmlessly, so she thinks. When the people complain to the rabbi about her careless and untrue words, he asks the woman to take his pillow, go to the roof, and cut open the pillow, and shake it so hard that the feathers fly out. When she has completed that task, the rabbi asks her to go back and gather up the feathers. "But I can't do that, Rabbi.

The feathers have flown away on the wind." The rabbi replies, "So too with words. Once they are released, they cannot be taken back." This is a favorite European folktale that has also been attributed to Rabbi Levi Yitzhak of Berditchev. Versions of this "gossip" story are in Molly Cone's *Who Knows Ten?*, which illustrates the ninth commandment: "Thou shalt not bear false witness against your neighbor"; and as a musical version, "Feathers," by Heather Forest in *Chosen Tales*, edited by Peninnah Schram.

The second story is a Talmudic tale about various parts of the body, including the tongue, that argue that each one is the most powerful. When a king becomes ill, the doctors find that the only remedy to cure him would be the milk of a lioness. One brave young man finds a lioness and, through a clever plan, manages to get the needed remedy. But when he returns to the palace, he tells the king, "I have the remedy that will cure you—it is the milk of a dog!" The king becomes furious and orders that the young man to be hanged. The parts of the body tremble with fear and ask the tongue that misspoke to save them. The tongue replies: "You see what has taken you days and days to accomplish [the getting of the milk], I have been able to undo in one second and with one word. Admit that I'm the most powerful, and I will save you." You can imagine how quickly the parts of the body said, "Yes, O tongue, you are the most powerful!" The lesson that we must use our words wisely comes through clearly and dramatically (AT 293*J: Debate of tongue and other bodily members). A version of this story, "The Great Debate" is in Peninnah Schram's *Jewish Stories One Generation Tells Another*. Thus we can see how, in Judaic thought, words and actions have an intimate relationship. Additionally, words can build or destroy relationships.

In the Israel Folktale Archives, there is a variant of this story told by Greek-Jews. "Wounds by an insult, unlike wounds by a dagger, will not heal" (IFA 10088), heard from Rachel Kabili, is printed in *The Golden Feather*, edited and annotated by Dov Noy. In this story, a rich merchant loses all his fortune. As he is about to drown himself, he plays his beloved violin one last time. A bear emerges from the water and throws the man a bag of pearls every day. Out of gratitude, the man invites the bear to his home. When his wife notices the dirt the bear leaves, she insults the bear. The bear asks the man to inflict on him some physical wounds. The bear teaches him that while the physical wounds can heal, insults are never forgotten. The bear disappears forever.

This is the most popular animal tale in the IFA, with sixteen versions as of 1976. For more analysis of this tale type, see Dov Noy's *Sipurey Ba'aley Hayim* (The Jewish Oral Animal Tale).

SOURCES AND VARIANTS
Mishle Shu'alim by Berechiah ha-Nakdan [in Hebrew].

"Lion and Hunter" in *Fables of a Jewish Aesop*, translated by Moses Hadas.

"Wounds by an insult, unlike wounds by a dagger, will not heal" in *The Golden Feather*, edited and annotated by Dov Noy.

The Folk Literature of the Kurdistani Jews: An Anthology by Yona Sabar.

Tale types: AT 159 B—Enmity of lion and man

AT 285 D—Serpent (bird) refuses reconciliation. (Reconciliation becomes impossible because each has injuries that cannot be forgotten.)

Motifs: B 857—Animal avenges injury.

W 185.6—Insult worse than wound

The Mouse That Went
Looking for a Husband

Berechiah ha-Nakdan lived in France in the thirteenth century. He collected fables that he rewrote in a way to interest Jewish readers. Like most fables, all his tales ended with a wise saying called a moral lesson. However, there is more than one moral to be found in these fables. Resourceful readers may want to think up their own lesson for this little tale about a little mouse.

A MOUSE FOUND A PLACE TO LIVE IN THE WALLS OF AN OLD synagogue. One day it was amazed when it peeked out of its hole and witnessed a beautiful Jewish wedding. The groom stood under a white cloth canopy. The bride walked around the groom seven times, and the groom led her under the white silk canopy. The rabbi chanted a blessing over a glass of wine. The bride and groom sipped the wine. Then the bride allowed the groom to place a golden ring on her finger. The wedding agreement was read aloud, and the couple was blessed. The groom stomped on the wine glass. When the glass broke with a loud noise, everybody shouted, "*Mazal tov!* Good luck!" Then came the wedding party with food and gifts, dancing, and singing. The bride was carried overhead on a chair like a queen on her throne.

The mouse said, "I want to get married, too." But she did not want to marry another mouse. "I want to marry someone better than a mouse," she said. "Mice are weak and fearful. I want to marry someone powerful." She asked her friends, the other mice, "Who is powerful?"

"The sun is powerful," said the other mice.

Mouse climbed to the highest roof in her little village, and she called out to the sun, "Sun, you shine above everything. You are very powerful."

The sun laughed and said, "I am not so powerful. Every night I must fall below the earth, and in the morning I must rise again. I can never stay in any one place. You should marry a mouse."

"No," said the mouse. "You shine over everything in the world."

"Ha!" laughed the sun. "The cloud covers me, and then I cannot shine at all."

"Then I will marry the cloud," said the mouse, and she called to the cloud. "Cloud, marry me. You are the most powerful one of all. You can block the sun that shines above everything."

The cloud just laughed and said, "I have no power to move or even to stay still. The wind pushes me everywhere."

So the mouse called to the wind, "Wind, marry me. You are the most powerful being in the world. You can push the cloud that blocks the sun that shines above everything."

The wind laughed and whispered in the mouse's ear, "I seem powerful as long as nothing stands against me, but as soon as I meet a wall I am stopped."

There was an ancient castle outside the mouse's village, and that castle had a huge wall around it. So the mouse went to the wall and said, "Wall, marry me. You are so powerful and mighty you can stop the wind that blows the clouds that blocks the sun that shines above everything."

The wall did not laugh. Instead, it cried, "Why have you come to tease me in my weakness?"

"How can a wall be weak? You are thick and high and made of solid stone," said the mouse.

"Your people, the mice, have dug thousands of tunnels under me. When it rains, the water pours down their tunnels and washes away the earth. The ground beneath me is collapsing. I am sinking and cracking. Some day I will fall and become a pile of rubble. Those weak and fearful mice have the power to break the wall that stops the wind that blocks the sun that shines above everything. Go marry a mouse."

And so she did.

The moral lesson of Berechiah ha-Nakdan: If you run after honor and power, you will fail. Don't try to be more than who you are.

NOTE

In 1200, when ha-Nakdan was collecting his fables, every book had to be copied by hand. This made books very expensive. After the printing press was invented, after 1465, many more books could be made and at a lower cost. Not only could more people afford to buy the books, but more people learned to read these stories. The unfortunate side was that people became used to reading stories in books, and eventually they stopped listening to storytellers.

ABOUT THE JEWISH WEDDING CEREMONY

Traditionally the bride walks around the groom seven times as they stand under the wedding canopy. In Jewish folk culture and magic, seven is associated with good luck. Thus, this custom probably derives from the folk belief in the protective power of the circle combined with the mystical and magical power of the number seven.

The white cloth canopy above the bride and groom represents a prayer shawl. In earlier times, the groom wrapped his prayer shawl around his bride to show that he would always protect her. The canopy also represents a tent. In Biblical times, a bride and groom would spend their wedding night in a special marriage tent.

Some say the groom breaks the wine glass after the ceremony to represent the destruction of the Temple. It reminds us that even though we may be happy, our lives will not be perfect until the Temple is rebuilt. Others think that breaking the glass represents the ending of one's unmarried life and the beginning of one's married life, or it makes us remember how fragile life can be. However, according to folk beliefs, the noise at the breaking of the glass scares off evil spirits and demons that are jealous of humans, especially at such happy occasions.

COMMENTARY

When I first read this fable, it reminded me of two similar cumulative tales, namely, "The Stonecutter" and "The Fisherman's Wife," both known in many cultures. A stonecutter wishes to be someone more powerful. His wish is granted, and he becomes transformed first into a rich man, then a king, then the sun, then a cloud, then the wind, and, finally, what he believes is the most powerful thing in the world, a mountain. One day, he suddenly feels something cutting into his base. Yes, it is a stonecutter with his ax. When he realizes that a stonecutter can chip away at stone, he wishes to become once again a stonecutter. It's a circular story, where the last element brings the character back to the circumstances he or she experienced at the beginning of the tale.

"The Fisherman's Wife" has a similar structure. A fisherman catches a magical fish, which grants a wish. His wife makes a total of six wishes, each one gaining more wealth and power: from hovel to cottage, to castle, to king, to emperor, to pope. For her sixth wish, when she requests to become God, the fish refuses. Instead, she is returned to the poor hovel where she started.

This fable is different in that the mouse wishes to marry something very powerful. However, the choices are parallel, especially to "The Stonecutter" story: the sun, cloud, wind, stone wall.

One of the sources for this story is *Kalilah ve-Dimnah*, which is a well-known collection of fables. Originally written in Sanskrit, this book was first translated into Persian, and then, in

750 C.E., into Arabic. It was then translated from Arabic into Hebrew, first by Jacob ben Eleazar (1195–1250) and later by Rabbi Joel in 1250. These wondrous tales, presented in a frame story by two jackals named Kalilah and Dimnah, served as a treatise on human nature for the princes of India, a sort of handbook for rulers. Interwoven with ethical sayings and proverbs, the fables and parables explore universal questions of truth and deceit, ambition and loyalty, fear and power. Containing many maxims from the Talmud and stressing Jewish values, the book was popular among the Jews of that time.

Along with Jacob ben Eleazar, Berechiah ha-Nakdan (about 1190 C.E.) was born in France, but while living in Oxford, he wrote 107 "fox fables" (*Mishle Shu'alim*). Many of his fables can be traced to Aesop, and some to Romulus collections, while others are similar to the work of Marie de France. However, ha-Nakdan has been called the Jewish Aesop. His foxes echo talmudic discussion and quote biblical sources, with the goal always to give lessons in social behavior rather than to teach religion.

SOURCES AND VARIANTS
Mishle Shu'alim (The Fox Fables of Berechiah ha-Nakdan).
　　"Mouse, Sun, Cloud, Wind, Wall" in *Fables of a Jewish Aesop*, translated by Moses Hadas.
　　Kalilah ve-Dimnah, edited by J. Derenbourgue.
　　Two versions, both titled "The He-Mouse and the She-Mouse," in *Mimekor Yisrael* by Micha Joseph Bin Gorion.
　　"The Mouse Seeks a Wife" in *The Classic Tales: 4,000 Years of Jewish Lore* by Ellen Frankel.

　　Tale Type: AT 2031—Stronger and strongest
　　Motifs: L 392—Mouse stronger than wall, wind, mountain
　　Z 42—Stronger and strongest

Teaching a Wolf

Some people have what is called a "one-track" mind. They can think of only one thing/idea/action and relate only to that thing/idea/action, no matter what else they are shown or experience. Can a person, or an animal, ever learn to go beyond his own personal instincts or interests? See what you think after you read this story.

A GREAT TEACHER OVERHEARD SHEPHERDS COMPLAINING ABOUT a dangerous wolf.

One said, "Most wolves leave my sheep alone. But one wolf tries to steal my sheep every night."

"It has eaten many of my sheep already," said the other.

The teacher said, "I will teach that wolf how to read and write. Then it will not have to kill sheep. It will find proper work and become a useful member of society."

The man found the wolf and visited him every day with food until the wolf trusted him completely. Then he began to teach the wolf to read. Every day he taught the wolf a letter of the Hebrew alphabet: *aleph, bet, gimel,* and *daled,* which are *A, B, C,* and *D.* He was such a good teacher that the wolf could name each letter—*A, B, C, D*—all the way through the alphabet. The teacher was overjoyed. He then combined the letters into words.

"Now, Wolf," said the teacher. "Read this word." The teacher put the letters *C-A-T* together, and the wolf said, "Sheep." The teacher tried again. He put the letters *D-O-G* together, and the wolf said, "Sheep." He tried again with the letters *S-U-N* and then with *S-K-Y,* but each time the wolf said, "Sheep."

"What is wrong with you?" the teacher asked. "No matter what I show you, you always answer, "Sheep."

"I don't understand it, either," said the wolf. "No matter what I try to think about, Sheep are always on my mind."

The teacher gave up. "That wolf cannot learn. It is like certain people who have only one thing on their minds. Some people think only about *M-O-N-E-Y*. Some think only of *P-O-W-E-R*. Some others think only about *F-A-M-E*. People like that think only about what they want for themselves, and they will never learn anything else."

NOTE
This fable may not be fair to wolves or to people. Recently, some troublesome wolves have been taught to stop attacking sheep. They hunt in the wild and leave sheep and other farm animals alone. Perhaps even people who think only about money, power, or fame can also change.

COMMENTARY
The moral of the story, placed at the beginning of the fable in *Fables of a Jewish Aesop*, is "A man whose eye and heart are bent on gain, his mouth declares his wickedness." Through a non-threatening, humorous fable about animals, the reader can gain a perspective and, thus, understand an important lesson about life and relationships. This is why fables are known as teaching tales.

SOURCE
"Man and Wolf" in *Fables of a Jewish Aesop* (Fox Fables of Berechiah ha-Nakdan), translated by Moses Hadas.

Tale Type: AT 1539—Cleverness and gullibility
Motif: K 112.1—The teaching of languages

What Do You Want to Be?
A Tale of Wisdom

Gluekel (1646–1724) lived in Hamelin, Germany. She did not have an easy life. She witnessed wars, plagues, and personal tragedies. Her husband died in an accident while traveling as a merchant, and she was left with thirteen children to care for. She took over her husband's work. She produced and sold merchandise while still taking care of her family. Even in times of tragedy, she had to work long hours every day.

Her life was also difficult because she was Jewish. Jews had to pay to enter the country. They even had to pay to be allowed to work. They were forced to live in cramped ghettos and were often falsely accused of crimes. She saw many of her people massacred in nearby Poland, and she helped take care of the survivors.

Nevertheless, Gluekel was thankful for all she had and for her many loving friends and family. Gluekel's Jewish faith made her life difficult but it also gave her strength.

As Gluekel grew older, she wrote the story of her life for her children and her grandchildren. She added her thoughts, her feelings, and the wisdom she had gathered over the years, along with special stories that had given her hope and inspiration. This is one of those stories.

JOSEPH WAS SHAKING HIS HEAD AS HE WALKED DOWN THE STREET. When he saw Sara, the old water carrier, he sighed loudly, "Oh, Sara," he said, "the only luck I ever have is bad luck."

"What's the matter?" asked Sara.

"I fail at everything!" cried Joseph. "I tried fishing, but all I caught was a cold! I tried farming, but all I grew were blisters on my hands. No, that's not true. I also grew tired, I grew poor, and I grew older, but I couldn't grow a potato or an onion or a single green bean!"

"You're young and healthy and well liked," said Sara. "Do you really think your life is bad?"

"It's worse," said Joseph. "I started a business and tried to sell umbrellas. But look at the sky! It hasn't rained for months! I always fail. If I sold lamps the sun would never set! If I sold gravestones, no one would ever die! Nobody has a worse life than me!"

Sara rested her hand on her young friend's shoulder. She said, "I am going up the mountainside. I want to fill my barrel where the stream runs clear and clean. Come with me and fill a barrel for yourself."

Joseph and Sara walked the winding path up the mountain. They came to an icy stream and filled their barrels with water. Then they had a good long drink. They sat and rested, watching the water flowing down the mountain, turning into a waterfall and then into a pond that joined the river flowing past the town.

Sara said, "When I was young, I played beside the river and ran along its banks. When I married, I went to work, drawing water from the river to carry into town. I worked alongside my husband, and now that he has died, my children work alongside me. We bring water to all the houses in the town, and I know every person who lives in every house."

Joseph laughed bitterly. "Ha! I wish I were one of those people. I wish I were anyone but me."

"Pick a house," said Sara, "I will tell you who lives there. Then you can decide whom you want to be."

Joseph pointed to a grand mansion in the finest part of town. "A rich person must live there."

"The man who lives in there is very rich," said Sara, "but he is also very lonely. Instead of coming home to a loving family, he comes home to a silent house. Instead of bringing friends, he brings the money he has earned that day. So it goes every day. He has no family and no friends. He eats from a golden plate and he drinks from a crystal glass, but he eats and drinks alone. Do you want to be him?" asked Sara.

"No," said Joseph. "I'd like to be rich but not lonely." Joseph picked a house with children in the yard and visitors heading to the door. "Look at all those people. Whoever lives there is never lonely."

"Yes, the woman who lives there is well loved," said Sara, "but she is sick and her family and friends stay close by to take care of her. She lays in bed day and night worrying. She worries about how to get better, and she worries about being a burden to her family and friends. The more she worries, the sicker she gets. Do you want to be her?"

"No," said Joseph. "I want friends and family around me but not because I am sick."

Joseph pointed to a house that was especially clean, tidy, and well cared for. "That house looks perfect. That person's life must be perfect as well," said Joseph.

"Nothing in that house is out of place except the hearts of those who live inside. The man is a great success, but he does not love his work. His heart was set on being something. His wife is admired for her good deeds, for her beauty, and for her fine character, but she does not love her husband. Both the man and woman in that house are sick at heart because they do not have what they truly want. Do you want to be either of them?"

"No, their lives are not perfect," said Joseph. "Their lives are perfectly awful."

Joseph kept picking houses, but he could not find one person without a problem. Some people felt they were too young or too old, too busy or not busy enough. Others were missing someone or yearning to be somewhere or craving for some thing. Many were troubled by the past and fearful about the future. No one's life seemed perfect, not even easy.

Joseph was silent for a long while, watching the river as it flowed past the town and wound its way toward the sea. Finally he stood up and said, "I've made my choice. I choose to be myself. I don't want to be anyone else. I have plenty of problems, but at least they are my own problems and I am used to them."

"That's how I feel, too," said Sara. She rubbed the muscles of her gnarled hands. Joseph saw the pain in Sara's face, and he understood that she had troubles of her own. "Who knows?" said Sara. "We may learn something from our troubles. Maybe we will even learn how to be happy."

A cool breeze stirred the grass. Birds began to gather in the trees. The day was ending. Joseph helped Sara to her feet, and together they watched the sun setting over the town, giving every house a golden glow.

The two of them turned to each other and smiled as good friends do. Then they lifted their full and heavy barrels onto their shoulders, and they walked down the path toward their separate homes, singing a song of praise.

NOTE

Abraham Ibn Ezra of twelfth-century Spain was famous not only for his biblical scholarship and penitential poetry but also for his misfortunes. He was able to laugh at his misfortunes by writing: "If I sold shrouds, no one would die. If I sold lamps, the sun would never set." Another popular Jewish saying is, "If I sold hats, people would be born without heads."

COMMENTARY

One of the eminent Jewish matriarchs of the mid-seventeenth and eighteenth centuries, Glueckel of Hamelin wrote her memoirs to ease her sorrow after the death of her husband. But she addressed the memoirs to her children, to teach them, without seeming to preach, about life and about leading a moral Jewish life. It was, in essence, an "ethical will." Glueckel began her memoirs as if "talking" to her children: "We should, I say, put ourselves to great pains for our children, for on this the world is built."

Jews have very colorful ways of expressing ideas, as we can see from the quote of Abraham Ibn Ezra (above). In fact, there are books filled with Yiddish expressions that are creatively original in their use of imagery and metaphor. The theme in this story is a popular Yiddish saying: "If you could hang on the wall all the world's packs of troubles, everyone would grab for his own" (quoted in *Words Like Arrows*, compiled by Shirley Kumove). I recall hearing my own mother say "If everyone threw his troubles into the sea and could draw out an equal share, everyone would prefer to take his own troubles back." Same idea! At least our own problems are familiar to us, so the reasoning goes, and it could always be worse.

Helen Mintz heard a similar story from an elder at a senior center who had heard it from her mother in Europe. It is "The Pekl Story" (a *pekl* means a small pack, in Yiddish), which is included in *Chosen Tales*, edited by Peninnah Schram.

There is an Arabic story about a father who goes out hunting with his son. Suddenly he realizes that his son had been killed by a gazelle. He carries his son home and tells his wife, "I have brought you back a gazelle [meaning their son], dear wife, but as God is my witness, it can be cooked only in a cauldron that has never been used for a meal of sorrow." When the wife inquires for such a pot from all her neighbors, she discovers every household has had a sorrow. The wife sadly concludes, "They have all tasted their share of sorrow. Today the turn is ours." (See "The Bedouin's Gazelle" in Inea Bushnaq's *Arab Folktales*.)

SOURCES AND VARIANTS
Retold from *The Memoirs of Glueckel of Hamelin*, translated by Marvin Lowenthal.
  This story is also excerpted in *In the Jewish Spirit*, edited by Ellen Frankel.

Sharp as a Diamond

Centuries ago in countries like Holland, there were no schools to learn skills. A young person had to become an apprentice to a master and hope the master would share his knowledge. Apprentices had to work hard to prove themselves.
But how do you prove that you can learn to cut a diamond?

DOV SPENT TWO YEARS WORKING FOR HIS MASTER, THE BEST diamond cutter in all of Holland. But his master would not teach him how to cut or polish diamonds or even how to set them into a ring or a necklace. The master kept Dov busy by having him sweep the workshop and sharpen the tools and deliver messages.

One day Dov asked his master, "When will you teach me how to work with diamonds?"

His master frowned and told him. "When you're smart enough. The mind of a diamond cutter has to be as sharp as a diamond."

He took out a large diamond in a golden ring. "Watch this," he said, and scraped the diamond against the window, etching the letters of his name upon the glass. He said, "This is the hardest, clearest, and sharpest diamond that I have ever had. It came all the way from India. I've cut it, polished it, and set it into this ring for a wealthy lord. Your job is to take it to him. Be careful, because it is worth more than you will ever earn in your whole life."

Dov hid the diamond ring in a leather traveling bag. He waited until it was dark and the streets were almost deserted. Then, when he thought no one would see him, he headed toward the lord's country mansion. He didn't realize that he was being watched and followed by a robber from the moment he left his master's shop. He was on a dark, deserted road when suddenly the robber leaped out of the bushes and blocked his way.

The man snarled, "You work for a diamond merchant, and you're hiding something in that bag. Hand it over."

Dov saw that the fellow was not very big or strong. He asked, "Why should I? What makes you so dangerous?"

"These two friends of mine," said the robber, and he pulled out a pair of pistols.

Dov quickly handed over the diamond ring, but as the robber turned to leave, Dov said, "You can't go yet. My master will call me a coward for giving up without a fight."

"But I have two pistols," said the robber.

"He won't believe it," said Dov. "Not unless I can show him the bullet holes."

"Are you asking me to shoot you?" said the robber.

"No, just shoot my jacket," said Dov, taking off his jacket and holding it up.

"Certainly!" said the robber with a nasty grin, and he blasted Dov's jacket right out of his hands.

"How about my hat?" said Dov, raising it in the air.

"With pleasure!" laughed the thief, and he shot Dov's hat to bits.

"Now shoot my traveling bag," said Dov, and he held out his bag. The thief aimed both pistols and pulled the triggers, but nothing happened.

"Are you out of bullets?" asked Dov.

"I suppose I am," said the robber, with a look of surprise.

"Now what makes you so dangerous?" Dov asked. He grabbed the robber's pistols and threw them down, then he grabbed the diamond ring and stuck it in his pocket. He was about to grab the robber, but the robber turned and ran.

Dov let him go. He delivered the diamond ring safe and sound to the wealthy lord. When he returned to his master, he told him everything that had happened.

The master smiled for the first time. He said, "Don't worry about your hat and coat. I'll buy you new ones. After all, a smart fellow like you should have a smart new outfit."

"How smart do you think I am?" asked Dov.

The master answered, "I'd say that you've got a mind as sharp as a diamond." And he taught Dov how to work with diamonds, which was what Dov had always wanted.

NOTE
When the Jews of Spain and Portugal were expelled (in 1492 and 1496), they searched for new homes. Arab countries accepted them, but of all the European countries, it was only Holland that truly welcomed them and gave them the full rights of citizens.

Holland was a "Land of Hope" for the Jews. Amsterdam began to be called "Mokum," meaning "the place" in Hebrew. This appellation is used by everyone in Amsterdam to this day. It was a great trading nation, with ships that sailed across the world. Some Jews became traders. Some learned to build newly invented instruments, such as clocks, eyeglasses, and telescopes. Others learned to cut and polish diamonds.

COMMENTARY
This is a universal tale found in Lithuanian, Flemish, Dutch, German, Russian, Korean, Spanish-American (U.S.), and Scottish folklore.

However, the encounter of the robber and a how-to-save-my-skin, quick-thinking Jew has also been told as an anecdote. Humor and laughter have often saved the Jews, at least psychologically if not always physically.

SOURCE AND VARIANTS
IFA 9899—"The Jew and the Robber" was collected by Shelomo Laba (Jerusalem) from his mother, Esther Lyubitsh (Russia). It can be found in *A Tale for Each Month 1973*, edited by Aliza Shenhar.

Tale Type: AT 1527A—Robber induced to waste his ammunition, then seized
Motifs: K 631.2—Disarming by a shooting test
K 724—Dupe induced to waste his bullets, then seized

Give Her What You Want

England in the 1600s was open to trade and travel. It was a time of exploration and discovery. Some Jews became sailors and traders, sailing to Africa, America, the Caribbean, and the Far East. Whatever they did, one skill remained most important: the ability to read well. Here is a tale that tests Malka's ability to read very carefully.

MALKA HAD BEEN TAKING CARE OF HER HOME AND HER CHILDREN without her husband for over a year. Her husband had been working as a trader in an English colony across the great Atlantic Ocean. He saved his money and sent it home to Malka whenever he could. Unfortunately, there were few ships sailing back to England. The money was almost gone. The children were hungry. Malka was getting desperate.

Then she heard a knock at the door. She and the children ran to answer it. A sea captain stood outside in high black boots and a wide-brimmed hat. He said, "I've come from the colonies. I've brought something from your husband."

Malka and the children welcomed him inside and crowded around as he opened a heavy money box. They were overjoyed when they saw that it was full of golden shillings. But the captain took out only ten and handed them to Malka.

"Is that all?" she asked. "My husband has been working for a year. He would have sent us far more than this."

"That's all you get," he said. "It was hard and dangerous to carry money such a long way. I took a share for my trouble."

"How much did you take?" asked Malka.

"What's the difference?" said the captain, walking to the door. "I've given you what I agreed to. I'm an honest man."

Malka stood in the doorway so that he couldn't leave, and she said, "If you are honest, as you say you are, then tell me what you took."

The captain looked uncomfortable, but finally he said, "I took ninety shillings."

"Robber!" she cried. She called the police, the neighbors, anyone else who would listen. Very quickly, Malka, her children, and the captain were in front of the Council of Judges.

"This woman does not understand business," the captain told the judges. "Her husband needed to send her money as soon as possible. I was the only person he could trust."

"What gives you the right to take so much of it?" asked the judges.

The captain answered, "It is my payment. Her husband did not want to pay so much, but finally he told me that I could give her what I want and I could keep the rest. He wrote it down in black and white."

The captain placed her husband's letter on the table. The letter read: "The captain agrees to deliver a box with one hundred shillings to my wife. He will give her what he wants, and he will keep the rest." The letter was signed by her husband.

The captain sneered, "I gave her ten shillings. I kept the other ninety. The letter proves I am honest."

Malka said, "It only proves that you are greedy man, which is almost as bad."

The captain shouted, "It is not my fault that your husband is a fool!"

Malka grew angry and shouted back, "My husband is no fool! He would never let you cheat me." When some people get angry they feel too upset to think, but when Malka got angry she thought even harder. She read the letter a second and then a third time. Suddenly she understood what her husband's words really meant.

She asked the captain, "Are you saying that you want ninety of those one hundred shillings?"

"Yes," said the captain.

Malka lowered her head so he could not see her smile. She asked quietly, "Please write it down in black and white."

The captain wrote, "I want ninety shillings," and signed his name.

"Good," said Malka. "Now give me ninety shillings."

"What do you mean?" he asked.

"Read my husband's letter," said Malka. "It says that you shall give me 'what you want' and you say in your letter that what you want is ninety shillings. So you must give me ninety shillings. It's written down in black and white."

The captain read and reread both letters. He yelled and stamped his feet, but finally he gave Malka the ninety shillings. Then he stormed out of town and off to sea, never to return.

Malka and her children took the money home. She immediately wrote to her husband saying how clever he was. The children also wrote to him saying how clever Malka was. In the next letter they received from him, he wrote saying that they were all clever and that he was coming home on the next boat.

NOTE

When the Jews lost their homeland, they no longer had their own king or a high priest (*kohen gadol*) to tell them how to live. They never knew when they would have to flee and be separated from their families and community. All important knowledge and laws had to be written down and preserved in books that people could carry with them. So every Jewish person had to learn to read and write. Reading was also a very useful skill that motivated some countries to accept Jews as immigrants.

The ability to read and write does not seem unusual now, but in earlier times it was rare. Generally, only priests and scribes who kept official records could read and write. In Europe, even the nobility was illiterate. A king signed documents by pressing his signet ring onto melted wax. By the 1400s, reading and writing became more common, but it was not until the past few hundred years that public schools were created to teach reading and writing to everyone. In America, the common school, the precursor to the public elementary school, began in New England and developed most significantly between 1820 and 1850. Public high schools gained in acceptance only in the late 1800s.

COMMENTARY

This is a story about interpreting the key words rather than taking them at face value. At first, the confused reader may miss the point of the story so that it may take several readings. The key word is "give as much as he wants" rather than "take as much as he wants." Thus, whatever the captain wishes for himself, he must then give to the wife. Very clever reasoning on the part of both the husband and wife!

In the version in *101 Jewish Stories*, edited by Simon Certner, it is the rabbi who catches the clue of give versus take in the husband's letter. In folktales, there is usually no specific setting for the story and no identified city where the traveling husband/merchant goes. However, in the version in this book, the reteller sets the story in England and America to teach some history of the Jewish journeys.

As with many folktales, it is the reasoning of a clever woman who solves the problem or interprets the riddle.

SOURCES AND VARIANTS

IFA 9706 - "Two Thirds" was collected by Malka Cohen from Rachel Avigdory from the *Ukraine in Mipi Haham* [in Hebrew] by Malka Cohen.

"Triumph over the Greedy" in *101 Jewish Stories*, edited by Simon Certner.

Tale Type: AT 926*E-I—As Much as He Wants

The Rich Man's Reward

If you were to find a bag of money or a wallet without identification, how would you go about finding its owner? How would a judge be able to determine the rightful owner? In this story, you will discover a clever way of reasoning in order to arrive at a just judgment—to reward honesty and punish deception and greed.

A GIRL NAMED ESTER WAS COMING INTO TOWN AT HARVEST TIME. It was a busy time of the year, and crowds of people were heading to the marketplace to buy and sell. Ester noticed a small leather bag on the ground. It was a plain leather bag, the kind that many people carried. When she looked inside, she found a hundred gold coins. She stared hard at the coins and shut the bag. She wanted to hide it under her jacket and run home. She thought of everything she could buy with so much money. Then she thought, "No. This is not mine. Someone lost it. I have to return it to its owner."

It was not difficult to find out who had lost it. Barak, the richest man in town, was standing outside his store telling everybody, "I've lost a bag of gold. I'll give half the money to whoever brings it back. Half the money!"

Everyone was rushing about looking for the bag. The whole town was in an uproar.

"I've found your money," said Ester. At first, Barak didn't hear the girl. He was too busy talking to adults. Finally, Ester held up the bag in front of Barak's face and shouted, "Here's your money!"

When Barak saw the bag he grabbed it out of Ester's hand. Everyone else congratulated Ester for being so honest. "You'll get half the money as a reward," they said. "Isn't that true, Barak?"

Barak said nothing. He just held the bag tightly.

"Count the money, Barak," they said.

Barak counted out the coins very slowly as everybody watched, but when he finished counting, he stared hard at the coins and shut the bag. He said, "There's something wrong. There are only one hundred coins in this bag. There should be two hundred."

People whispered to each other. "Maybe Ester is not honest after all. Maybe she took half the money for herself, and now she is trying to get even more!"

Ester blushed. She said, "All the coins are there. I didn't take a thing."

"First you steal, and now you lie," said Barak. "You can keep the one hundred coins you took. That was going to be the reward. But you won't get any more from me."

"It's not true, and it's not fair," said Ester. She wanted to run away, but now she had to stay to prove she wasn't dishonest.

Everyone was talking, but no one knew what to do until someone went to get Reb Cohen. Reb Cohen always knew what to do and how to do it.

When Reb Cohen arrived, he asked, "What is the problem?"

Barak shouted out, "That girl is a thief and a liar."

Reb Cohen asked the people, "Has the girl ever stolen or lied before?"

The people said, "No, she's always been fine and decent." Then they thought about Barak, and they remembered things that he had done that were not at all fine or decent.

Barak scowled and said, "I lost a bag with two hundred gold coins."

Ester said, "I found this bag, but it had only one hundred coins."

Barak turned to Reb Cohen and said angrily, "You decide. Who are you going to call dishonest, me or that girl?"

Reb Cohen looked carefully at Barak and then at Ester. "I don't need to call anyone anything," said Reb Cohen. "Barak lost a bag with two hundred coins. Ester found a bag with one hundred coins. Obviously, the bag that Ester found is not Barak's."

"What!" Barak sputtered.

Reb Cohen ignored him and put his hand on Ester's shoulder. He said, "You are a fine and decent person, Ester. Since no one claims to have lost a bag with one hundred coins, it now belongs to you."

He gave the bag to Ester, and everybody cheered because Ester got what she deserved and so did Barak.

NOTE

There are many tales of a clever judge who sometimes must find a way to interpret the law so that true justice is served. One story takes place at Sukkot, a Jewish harvest festival, when people spent seven days and nights in specially built temporary huts called *sukkahs*. Instead of an ordinary roof, the beams were hung with harvested fruit and vegetables, then covered with pine branches or other branches with leaves so that the stars would be visible. Living and sleeping in the sukkah reminds Jews of how they used to work and sleep in the fields during the harvest time in Israel. It also commemorates the temporary dwellings of the Israelites as they wandered in the desert for forty years after leaving Egypt but before arriving in the Promised Land.

It was hard to celebrate Sukkot in a big city. However, one man built a sukkah on the balcony of his apartment. This angered the landlord. He wanted it taken down immediately. They went to court, and the Jewish tenant explained the importance of having a sukkah during the seven days of Sukkot.

The judge said, "The landlord has the law on his side. You are not allowed to build a hut on his balcony. However, there are many ways of obeying the law." The judge winked and gave his clever judgment. "I order you to take down the sukkah within seven days."

COMMENTARY

In Nathan Ausubel's version in *A Treasury of Jewish Folklore*, it is a *schlimazl* (an unlucky puerson) who finds the money lost by the richest man of the town. However, the rich man always uses his conniving reasoning in a way to cheat the finder out of his just reward. In most versions, the rabbi or, in this case, the judge finds the wisdom to resolve the dilemma, leaving the rich man with nothing.

"Honesty is the best policy."

SOURCES AND VARIANTS

A version of this story is in *Mipi Haham* by Malka Cohen.

"Triumph over the Greedy" in *101 Jewish Stories*, edited by Simon Certner.

A variant is "Too Clever Is Not Clever" in Nathan Ausubel's *A Treasury of Jewish Folklore*.

"The Finder Gets His Reward" is in *101 Jewish Stories*, edited by Simon Certner.

The Shepherd's Pipe

Most of the time we think that wisdom comes from the mind, but there is also a wisdom of the heart. This is a tale of that kind of wisdom.

ON THE EVE OF YOM KIPPUR, THE DAY OF ATONEMENT, A SHEPHERD entered a synagogue with his son. The boy had spent his whole life in the distant hills herding sheep with his father. He had never been taught to read or write. He knew nothing about being Jewish. He had never even been to town before.

"Father," he asked, "What is this place?"

"It is a place to pray," said his father.

"What does pray mean?" he asked.

"It means to speak so God can hear you."

"But God hears everything," said the boy.

"Then, be quiet," said his father. He led the boy to a seat at the back of the synagogue, and he handed him a prayer book.

"I can't read this," said the boy.

"It doesn't matter," said the father. "Pretend to read and pretend to sing the prayers. Just do what everyone else does."

"They don't sound as if they are praying or singing. They are mumbling and groaning and whispering," said the boy. "Are they just pretending?"

"Don't ask silly questions," said the father.

At that moment, the rabbi lifted up a ram's horn and blew it with all his might.

"Who is that man?" the boy asked.

"That is the great Rabbi Israel, the *Baal Shem Tov,*" replied the father.

"Why did he blow that ram's horn?" the boy asked.

"He is trying to get our prayers to fly up to Heaven," said the father impatiently.

"I can help him," said the boy as he took his shepherd's pipe from his pocket.

"That's against the rules!" his father said. The boy felt frightened, so he put away the pipe. He pretended to read and sing just as his father had told him to do. But the more he pretended, the more tired and bored he felt. Then he saw Rabbi Israel lift the ram's horn again, and he heard him blow it loud and strong. He pulled his father's sleeve and said, "Father, I can't read a prayer or sing a prayer, but I can blow a prayer with my pipe."

"What's wrong with you?" said the father. "I told you to put that thing away." The boy felt ashamed, and he put it back in his pocket.

At the end of the day, the sun was setting, and the room grew dark. Even Rabbi Israel looked tired and sad as he picked up the ram's horn to blow it for the last time.

"I have to play my pipe," said the boy. He pulled it from his pocket, but his father grabbed his hand.

"You don't know what you're doing!" said the father. "You'll be in big trouble." They struggled with the pipe, but finally the boy pulled it free and blew a long high note with all his might. At that same moment the rabbi blew the ram's horn, and the two sounds joined together. The father was too upset to even look at his son. The service ended, and the rabbi approached them.

"I am very embarrassed," said the father.

Rabbi Israel said to the father, "You did what you thought was right. You just didn't understand."

"Will you forgive me?" the father asked.

Rabbi Israel said, "Don't ask me for forgiveness; ask your son."

"Why?" asked the father in bewilderment.

"Because you almost stopped his prayer," the rabbi said.

The rabbi patted the shepherd boy on the shoulder and said, "Thank you for blowing on your pipe. The people's prayers were weak and scattered. I tried to lead them with my prayers and the *shofar,* but I could not do it by myself. When you blew your pipe, the sound joined the blast of my ram's horn. The two sounds formed such a powerful prayer, it reached Heaven's gate and led the way for all the others."

NOTE

The Days of Awe and Yom Kippur: The Days of Awe are the first ten days of the Jewish New Year, which occur in the fall at the beginning of the seventh month of the Jewish year. The first day is Rosh Hashanah, which means "head of the year." People pray in the synagogue. Then they gather for a family meal, and they wish each other a good year. During the Days of Awe, people are supposed to think about what they have done wrong during the past year and how to change for the better.

The final day of this period is Yom Kippur, the Day of Atonement. Adults go without food or water from sunset to sunset and spend the entire day in the synagogue praying for redemption. They accept responsibility for everything that they and their people have done wrong, and they ask forgiveness. The blasts of the ram's horn (shofar) help keep people alert and inspire them to pray.

The Jewish calendar: The standard calendar begins with the birth of Jesus. Using that calendar, this book was published in the year 2005. The Jewish calendar begins with the creation of the world (according to the Bible, it happened 3760 years earlier). Using the Jewish calendar, this book was published in the year 5765.

The Baal Shem Tov: Israel ben Eliezer (1700–1760) was also called the Baal Shem Tov, which means "Master of the Good Name." A follower of this rabbi is called a *Hassid* (meaning "pious one"). The *Hassidim* (plural) believe that he had mystical knowledge and could perform miracles. The Baal Shem Tov taught people that they could reach God through their feelings and intentions, especially through love and joy. In this famous story, which takes place in Poland, the pipe and shofar helped the rabbi and the boy to open everyone's hearts so that their prayers were able to reach God.

COMMENTARY

An international tale type, this story has variants told in Jewish, Christian, and Islamic cultures. This theme of an innocent and unlearned man praying to God in his own words, but directly from the heart, is especially popular in Jewish folktales. This comes from the saying *"Rakhmana lieba ba'ee"* (God wants the heart), which, according to folklorist Dov Noy, is based upon the Talmudic maxim in Sanhedrin 106b, which stems from I Samuel 17:7. In Psalms 116:6, there is also a reference to the simple man: "God guards the simple."

A similar version of this theme is about a child who does not know how to read the prayers. But as he sits in the synagogue and yearns to tell of his love for God, he begins to recite the Hebrew alphabet letters. When the learned grown-ups around him scold him for what he is doing, he explains: "I told God that while I didn't know how to read the prayers, I know how to recite the aleph-bet. And You, God, please take the letters and arrange them into prayers to say what is in my heart." At the end of the tale, it is clear that everyone understands something more deeply about the "right" way to pray, with the heart and from the heart.

In his book, *The Hasidic Anthology*, Louis I. Newman has two excerpts in his category "Children," which illustrate the "God Wants the Heart" motif: "The Baal Shem Tov said: 'The Lord does not object even if one misunderstands what a man learns, provided he only strives to understand out of his love of learning. It is like a father whose beloved child petitions him in stumbling words, yet the father takes delight in hearing him' "; and a note from Sholom Spiegel's *Hebrew Reborn*: "God loves not so much the man of learning and intelligence as the man of simple mind who artlessly and confidently puts all his faith in Heaven. Rabbi Nachman used this simile: 'As a father rejoices when his son makes his first halting steps and finds delight in him although he cannot walk, so the Holy One, blessed be He, finds delight in everyone in Israel who endeavors to fulfill a commandment'" (149).

SOURCES AND VARIANTS
Kehal Hasidim Hehadash, published in Lemberg in early nineteenth-century variants: *Sefer Hasidim MN* (Mekitse Nirdamim), ed. Yehuda Hacohen Wistynezki.

"The Prayer of the Shepherd" in *Mimekor Yisrael*, edited by Micha Joseph Bin Gorion.

"The Little Whistle" in *Tales of the Hasidim: Early Masters* by Martin Buber.

"The Shepherd's Pipe" in *Jewish Folktales*, retold by Pinhas Sadeh.

"The Yom Kippur Flute" in *The Classic Tales: 4,000 Years of Jewish Lore*, retold by Ellen Frankel.

"The Boy Who Could Only Play a Flute" in *101 Jewish Stories*, edited by Simon Certner.

"The Shepherd's Prayer" retold by Susan Danoff in *Chosen Tales*, edited by Peninnah Schram.

"The Shepherd" in *Days of Awe*, retold by Eric A. Kimmel.

"Only One" in *Folktales of Joha: Jewish Trickster*, collected and edited by Matilda Koen-Sarano. (In this story, the trickster Joha confuses the word "Echad" (one) with "Acher" (the other) in a prayer. Finally the rabbi realizes that it doesn't matter even if the "wrong" word is used as long as it is said with a pure heart.)

Tale Type: AT 827—A shepherd knows nothing of god
Motif: V 51.1—God wishes the heart

Don't Ask

Rabbis were responsible for everyone in their community. They often had to deal with serious problems, but they did not have the power of a policeman or a judge. Often, they had only the power of persuasion. In this two-hundred-year-old tale, a rabbi uses what is now called "reverse psychology" to change a stubborn man.

Reb Israel was a great teacher, respected by everyone in his town of Vishnitz, Poland. Every evening, he would walk with his students. People would greet him and ask for his advice or help.

ONE DAY REB ISRAEL STOPPED IN FRONT OF THE HOUSE OF A RICH banker. People never asked that banker for anything because whenever they did, he laughed at them and sent them away. In fact, he seemed to enjoy refusing to help people.

Reb Israel knocked on his door. The banker was surprised but invited him and his assistants inside. The banker chatted in a friendly way, waiting for Reb Israel to say why he had come. Instead Reb Israel smiled and nodded but said nothing. Finally, he thanked the banker for his time and rose to leave.

The banker said, "I'm sure you came to ask me for something. What is it?"

Reb Israel said, "I came to not ask you for something."

"What do you mean?" said the banker.

"There is a commandment that says, 'Ask for what you want only if you will be listened to. If you will not be listened to, then do not ask for what you want.' I wanted to fulfill the commandment of not asking. So I came to you because more than anyone in this whole town, you would not listen if I ask for what I want."

This made the banker curious. He said, "What do you want? If you ask, maybe I will listen."

"No, I am sure you won't," said Reb Israel, and he walked out of the house.

This made the banker even more curious. He followed the rabbi down the street, but Reb Israel refused to tell him anything. Finally, the banker begged for a hint about what the rabbi wanted. So Reb Israel said, "A poor old woman owes your bank a lot of money. Next week you are going to take her house to pay for her debt. She will be left homeless."

The banker said, "Don't say another word. There is no way I can help her."

"You see!" said Reb Israel. "You won't listen; that's why I won't ask."

The banker shook his head, saying, "I can't ignore her debt. She doesn't owe me the money; she owes the bank the money! I just manage the bank."

Reb Israel answered, "A clever man like you can find many reasons to say no," and he walked home.

The next day, the banker came to Reb Israel's house. He said, "My bank has to make people pay their debts, or else the bank would lose money. The bank would go bankrupt! That wouldn't be fair, would it?"

Reb Israel turned to his students and said, "Listen to how that man is refusing to listen."

The banker turned red in the face and sputtered, "I have to take her house. These are the rules of the bank. I have no choice!"

Reb Israel said, "Ha! I was waiting for you to say that you had no choice. Now I am certain that if I asked for what I want, you would not listen." He then led the banker out of his house.

The next day the banker came back. He hadn't slept, he hadn't eaten, he'd been pulling at his hair. He said, "Reb Israel, do you realize how much money that woman owes? It's a fortune!"

Reb Israel answered, "It doesn't matter whether she owes a lot or a little. You still would not listen."

"Stop saying that!" yelled the banker. "I'll pay her debt myself, but don't you ever ask me for anything again!"

Reb Israel smiled and shook the banker's hand. He said, "Congratulations, you're doing a very good deed. But why are you upset with me? I never asked you for anything."

The banker paid the debt, the old woman stayed in her house, and Reb Israel fulfilled the commandment of not asking.

NOTE

Commandments: Most people know about the Ten Commandments that Moses received on Mount Sinai. Soon afterward, the Jews (who were then called Israelites or Hebrews) received another 613 commandments. These commandments were more detailed directions about how to act and how not to act.

We are told that the 613 commandments include 248 positive statements about how to act. That number is equal to the 248 parts of the body. There are also 365 statements about how not to act. That number is equal to the 365 days of the year.

Two thousand years later, there were even more directions on how to live. They were written down in Babylon in the fifth century. That is where the commandment in this story comes from.

The actual commandment is written in the Babylonian Talmud (Yevamot 65b). It reads: "One is commanded to say what will be listened to. So, too, one is commanded not to say what will not be listened to."

Many commandments were rules about good and bad action, which everyone needs to understand. Other commandments were rules that applied only to the Jews, such as eating kosher food or observing the Jewish Sabbath. They are part of Jewish traditions, and they gave Jews a clear sense of identity. Jews needed a clear sense of who they were and what they believed, especially when they had to live as a minority in Christian and Muslim societies that had different customs and beliefs.

COMMENTARY

In Shlomo Yosef Zevin's *A Treasury of Chassidic Tales on the Torah*, the verse in Exodus 6:12, "The Children of Israel have not listened to me," serves as a springboard for this story. Reb Yisrael of Vizhnitz certainly used reverse psychology in order to reach the heart of the host/bank manager. By performing a *mitzvah*, Reb Yisrael offered another an opportunity to perform perhaps an even greater mitzvah.

Many rabbis became well known for helping people and also for helping rich misers, who gave grudgingly, if at all, to open their pockets and give charity. The Dubner Maggid had a most wonderful method of reaching the miserly rich, namely by telling them a parable. In this way, he opened their hearts as well as their purses. (For some of these stories, see Benno Heinemann's *The Maggid of Dubno and his Parables* and "The Maggid of Dubno" in *Stories Within Stories: From the Jewish Oral Tradition*, retold by Peninnah Schram.)

A story: Once the Dubner Maggid approached a wealthy man who never gave charity. He told the maggid that since everyone else gives, his contribution wouldn't make much impact, so why should he bother giving. The Dubner Maggid said, as usual, "Give me a moment and let me tell you a parable." And the rabbi told this wealthy man about a community that needed to raise some money to repair the synagogue. They placed a large barrel in the hallway, and every day, when the men would come for prayers, they would bring a bottle of their own wine to pour into the barrel. When the barrel was full, they would sell the wine for profit and be able to repair the roof. On the day of the sale, when they turned on the spigot, all that came out was water. It seemed that someone thought, "Why should I bring wine that I have worked hard to produce. I'll just bring a bottle of water that no one will notice, and it won't dilute this large barrel of wine." But it seemed that everyone had the same idea and no one brought the real wine. When the wealthy miser heard this story, he understood what it meant to be part of a community where each person can matter and make a difference. I leave it to you to decide whether or not he gave charity after all. A version of this wine/water story is "Interweaving Stories" in Peninnah Schram's *Jewish Stories One Generation Tells Another*.

SOURCES
"Time to Remain Silent" in Rabbi Shlomo Yosef Zevin's *A Treasury of Chassidic Tales on the Torah*, Vol. 1. Translated by Uri Kaploun.

"When to Say Nothing" is in *Jewish Wisdom* by Rabbi Joseph Telushkin and also under the category of "Rabbis" in his book *Jewish Humor*.

Motifs: P160—Beggars
V400—Charity

Changing a Mind

Throughout the centuries, governments did not take care of the poor or the sick. Instead, families and communities had to take care of their own. That was especially difficult for the Jews of Eastern Europe. Many were poor, and few were rich. Rabbis were always encouraging people to be charitable. They felt that charity improved the life of whoever received it, and it also improved the spirit of whoever gave it. Here are two tales of rabbis who found different ways of changing a mind and softening a heart.

A WEALTHY MISER REFUSED TO HELP ANYONE IN THE VILLAGE. THE rabbi came to visit and told the miser, "Look out your window." The man saw a street full of people. The rabbi then said, "Look in your mirror." The miser saw only himself.

The rabbi asked, "Your window and your mirror are both made of glass. What makes them different?"

The miser said, "The window glass is clear, so I can see outside. The mirror glass has a silver coating behind it. The silver stops me from seeing through. It reflects back so I see myself."

The rabbi said, "Your love for silver has changed your soul. Once, your soul was as clear as the glass of a window. You could look out at the world and see everyone. But you have coated your soul with silver. You no longer see anyone but yourself."

The miser understood. He was overcome with shame and changed his ways.

COMMENTARY

In a different version of this story, "Which Way Should One Look—Up or Down?" (in *Stories Within Stories: From the Jewish Oral Tradition*, retold by Peninnah Schram), I incorporate the idea of looking up at the sky to appreciate the world as well as through the window to see others, rather than just running to do business in the marketplace at the expense of experiencing life. This story also prompts me to remember Genesis 13:14, "And the Lord said unto Abram, 'Lift up now thine eyes, and look from the place where thou art, northward and southward and eastward and westward' " and again in Genesis 22:4, "On the third day Abraham lifted up his eyes . . ." To look up and see beyond ourselves are Jewish values and worthwhile goals.

SOURCES AND VARIANTS

Gemeinde der Chassidim by Chaim Bloch.

"The Mirror and Its Silver" in *The Hasidic Anthology*, compiled by Louis I. Newman. He credits this story to S. Ansky's play *The Dybbuk*.

"The Window and the Mirror" retold by Hannah Grad Goodman in *Lessons from Our Living Past*, edited by Jules Harlow.

"The Glass and the Mirror" in *101 Jewish Stories*, edited by Simon Certner

In the version of this story in Ellen Frankel's *The Classic Tales*, the rabbi who teaches the rich Jew the difference between the glass and the mirror is Rabbi Eisig of Ziditzov, and is included in the Hasidic Period section of that book.

Motifs: P160—Beggars
V 400—Charity

Softening a Heart

Another rabbi used a completely different method to teach the mitzvah of giving charity.

A RABBI ASKED A WEALTHY MAN TO GIVE CHARITY. THE MAN scornfully tossed him a penny. As the rabbi picked up the penny, he praised and thanked the wealthy man.

The rabbi's assistant asked, "How can you be so kind to such an unkind person?"

The rabbi answered, "That man has never given even a penny before now. I must encourage him even if he only gives a little. He needs to be taught how to be generous."

And so it happened. Each time the rabbi returned, the man gave a little bit more. Each time the rabbi praised and thanked him.

On the fourth visit, the man burst into tears, and to everyone's surprise, he gave the rabbi a tremendous sum. The rabbi was about to praise and thank him, but the man shook his head and said, "You deserve my praise and thanks, Rabbi, because you kept believing in me. You have taught me how to be generous."

COMMENTARY

There are many stories about charity (*tzedakah*), and there are many ways to teach the value of giving charity. Charity is one of the three foundations of the world (Avot 1:2). The Talmud delineates the importance and rationale for giving charity (as well as the punishments for those who do not). (See Baba Bathra 10a, 10b, and 11a, and Midrash Rabbah, Leviticus 34:10-11.) The philosopher Maimonides enumerated eight levels of giving charity, the highest being to help the needy person support himself in some occupation. Thus, helping someone in need is one of the greatest *mitzvot* (plural meaning "good deeds"). As it is written: "Charity saves from death" (Proverbs 10:2).

In Jewish oral and written traditions, there are numerous laws governing and promoting the giving of charity. For example, of all the many thematic sections in Louis Newman's *The Hasidic Anthology*, one of the longest list of stories is under "Charity."

On one hand, we have many stories that revolve around the cleverness of beggars and the impudence of such characters as *schnorrers*, tricksters, and other types of beggars. (See "The Poor People and Their Shares" in *Stories Within Stories: From the Jewish Oral Tradition*, by Peninnah Schram.) On the other hand, we also have the rabbis who appeal for monies in order to help others. Often, these rabbis, such as the Dubner Maggid, have to teach a wealthy miser to become more generous. "Softening a Heart" is such a story, which leads a wealthy man to gradually increase the amount of his giving.

Motifs: P 160—Beggars
V 400—Charity

The Coachman's Answer

In the 1700s and 1800s, many Jewish people lived in poor villages across Eastern Europe. Sometimes they went hungry, but most of all they hungered for knowledge. There was always great excitement when a traveling teacher, called a Maggid, came to share his knowledge. Here is a story about a highly respected teacher and his lowly coachman and how things suddenly changed.

MOTTL THE COACHMAN WAS DRIVING THE MAGGID OF DOBNO through the countryside as he often did. It was almost Purim, and the Maggid was traveling to a distant town to speak about the meaning of the holiday and to answer people's questions. The Maggid was a clever man, who enjoyed teaching people. Mottl was a cheerful man, who enjoyed driving his wagon, but on this day, Mottl was moody and depressed.

"What is wrong, Mottl?" the Maggid asked.

"I am unhappy," said Mottl.

"Why?" asked the Maggid.

"Because I wish I was you instead of me," said Mottl.

"Why?" the Maggid asked.

"You are a great teacher, and wherever we go, people are excited to see you. They crowd around you to listen to every word you say. They give parties in your honor, and they thank you for teaching them so much. But no one even notices me. It's not fair."

"Why not?" asked the Maggid.

"Because you are so learned, and I . . . I am Mottl," said Mottl. "Just once in my life, I wish I could feel clever, like a scholar."

"Would you be able to give a speech as I do?" asked the Maggid.

"I can give your speeches. I've heard them all a hundred times," said Mottl.

"Can you answer people's questions as I do?" asked the Maggid.

"I've heard your answers, too. It's so easy, so simple. I remember all of your answers so that even a wagon driver, like me, can do it."

"Fine!" said the Maggid. "I'll give you a chance to feel like a scholar. Today, I'll be the coachman and you will be the Maggid." They exchanged their hats and coats, and they switched places. The Maggid drove the horses and looked just like a coachman. Mottl sat beside him stroking his beard and looked just like a Maggid. When they got to the village, everyone cheered and waved at Mottl. Mottl smiled and waved back, just like a Maggid.

Thinking he was the Maggid, the people brought Mottl into a large study house, and they all crowded inside to listen to his speech. Suddenly Mottl felt nervous in front of so many people, but he also felt excited because this was his chance to feel learned, clever, and wise. He began giving the Maggid's speech. He said the same words as the Maggid. He sounded like the Maggid. He even moved his hands and nodded his head like the Maggid.

The speech was perfect. When Mottl finished, the people looked very impressed and raised their hands with questions, just as they did with the Maggid. Mottl remembered all the answers. Everything went splendidly until someone asked a question that Mottl had never heard before. He had no idea what to answer.

"That is an interesting question," said Mottl as his face turned red. "It is an unusual question," he said as his hands began to shake. Mottle looked around desperately for the Maggid to help him, but the Maggid was far away, standing at the very back of the room, looking as worried as Mottl felt.

People began to whisper, "What's wrong? Why isn't he answering the question? Is it possible that the great Maggid of Dubno doesn't know the answer?"

Mottl cleared his voice and said, "Of course I know the answer. I'll tell you why I am not answering. Because it's so easy. It's so simple that even my coachman can answer it." He pointed to the Maggid at the back of the room and said, "Coachman, answer the question!"

The real Maggid of Dubno breathed a sigh of relief and answered the question perfectly. Everyone was amazed. They said to Mottl, "You know so much, and even your coachman knows more than we do!"

The Maggid smiled at Mottl, and Mottl smiled back because Mottl finally felt very clever indeed.

NOTE

Education has always been very important to Jews. Because they did not have their own government or army like most people, they lived in whatever country accepted them. They never knew when they would suddenly be forced to leave or would lose their leaders.

To keep their identity, every Jewish person needed to be educated about being Jewish. They studied their books of wisdom and religion to understand and practice their traditions and beliefs. That was unusual at a time when few people in the world could even read. Some Jews became "rebbes," who were respected for their knowledge. Some acted as judges, others as teachers or scholars, and some took care of religious matters. A Maggid was a traveling preacher, who inspired the people by teaching the Bible in a way that everyone could understand, often through parables.

"The Coachman's Answer" is a great tale for Purim because Purim is a holiday of tricks, jokes, reversals, and disguises. It's a holiday that Jews celebrate with plays, carnivals, and costume parties. They change their identities with masks and costumes to feel what it is like to suddenly change who they are. It is a great way to understand the miracle of Purim, when powerful but evil people, like Haman, suddenly lost power, and the Jews, who were powerless, suddenly became strong and free.

Purim recalls a dangerous time in Persia (which is now called Iran). Haman, the king's advisor, convinced the king to let him kill all the Jews in the kingdom. However, Mordechai, a Jewish leader, secretly asked Ester, the king's wife, to save the Jews. Ester was secretly a Jew who had purposely not revealed her true identity. She convinced the king that Haman was his real enemy. The day that Haman was going to kill the Jews, the king issued a proclamation allowing the Jews to attack Haman and his supporters instead. The villains were all hanged, and the Jews of Persia were saved.

In the evening and the following afternoon of Purim, the story of Purim is read out loud from a scroll called the Megillah. When the people hear the name Haman, they whirl noisy clackers, called *groggers*, to drown out his name. Some write Haman's name on the soles of their shoes and stamp it out noisily. People also bake and eat *hamantaschen*, fruit-filled pastries shaped like Haman's three-cornered hat.

COMMENTARY

Many times, when a humorous folktale or a joke has been repeated over the years, the main character becomes a variable. In this story of a renowned rabbi and his driver, often the rabbi is the Dubner Maggid, sometimes Rabbi Eliahu of Chelm, or perhaps the Baal Shem Tov. Since there is no historical record of this incident actually happening, the identity of the rabbi is not the point. Nor is the point the deception perpetrated by the driver and the rabbi on the community. Rather, it is to focus on the humorous perspective and the point of the story; namely, to be careful about attributing too much adulation on any one person, no matter how learned, and also to illustrate that knowledge belongs to everyone, even a carriage driver. Thus, we must be careful how we judge people. But thanks to the quick wit of the driver, he was able to turn the tables on the challenge of the unfamiliar question and get out of a tight situation.

SOURCES AND VARIANTS
Under the category "The Sages of Chelm" in the *Encyclopedia of Jewish Humor: From Biblical Times to the Modern Age*, edited by Henry D. Spalding. Told with Rabbi Eliahu of Chelm as the scholar.

"The Peasant Who Pretended to Be a Rabbi" in *Lessons from Our Living Past*, edited by Jules Harlow.

Under "The Khukham in Jewish Humor" in Joseph Telushkin's *Jewish Humor*, the rabbi is the eighteenth-century Rabbi Yehezkel Landau of Prague.

Motif: J 1485—Mistaken identity

The Prince Who Thought He Was a Rooster

This is an allegorical story that can be understood on a literal but also symbolic level. It may be surprising to know that this is a Hasidic tale, since it involves a surprisingly humorous situation. Perhaps you are able to see yourself, or someone you know, in the character of the Prince.

THERE WAS A COUNTRY FULL OF PEOPLE WHO LOVED TO SHOW OFF. They would strut about in their finest clothes and brag as much as they could. Their prince was brilliant, brave, and handsome, so he got to show off and strut about and brag more than anyone.

However, the prince had a secret that bothered him more and more. Finally he became depressed. He sat, staring silently at the floor, day after day. Finally, during a great banquet, he jumped to his feet and shouted, "I cannot stand pretending anymore. I am not a brilliant, brave, and handsome prince! I'll tell you what I really am." He threw his food off the table, he tore his clothing off his body, and he announced, "I am a rooster!"

The prince gave a *cockel* and a *doodle-doo* and sounded like a rooster. He walked like a rooster. He even scratched the ground for bugs and seeds like a rooster.

Everybody shouted, "The prince is crazy!"

The king cried, "My son's a royal lunatic!" and he offered a fortune to anyone who could make him better.

The most important doctors came from everywhere and did everything they could. Nothing helped.

Then Joseph came to call. Joseph was not important to anybody. He was a Jewish peddler who bought broken watches, cracked pots and pans, and worn-out clothes to repair or sell for scrap. But when he saw the prince acting like a rooster, he told the king, "I can make him better."

The king was so desperate that he agreed. "You had better not fail, or else," said the king.

"Leave us alone for a week," said Joseph.

The first thing Joseph did was take off his clothes. He gave a *cockel* and a *doodle-doo* and sounded like a rooster. He walked like a rooster. He even scratched the ground for bugs and seeds like a rooster.

The prince watched him carefully but kept his distance. After three days, the prince became friendly with Joseph in a roosterly sort of way, and they shared their bugs and seeds.

The next day at sunrise, the prince began his crowing. Joseph said, "You have a terrific *cockle*, but you need to practice your *doodle-doo*."

The prince was so surprised he blurted out, "Roosters can't talk!"

"I happen to be a rooster who can talk. So can you. And why not?"

The prince thought it over. After a while he began to talk, though only about roosterly things. The next day at sunrise, Joseph gave a terrific *cockle-doodle-doo*.

"Hey," said the prince. "You walked like a person. Roosters can't do that."

Joseph smiled and said, "I happen to be a rooster who can walk like a person. I think you can, too. And why not?"

Soon the prince was walking in a graceful human way, just like Joseph.

The next day, Joseph put on his clothes. He said that he happened to be a rooster who wore clothes. The prince decided to wear clothes as well. And why not?

By the end of the week, they were both ordering human food from the royal menu.

"My son is a prince again!" cried the king, and everybody cheered and bowed to the prince.

"Why do they think I'm a prince?" the prince asked Joseph. "Don't they know that I'm a rooster?"

Joseph answered, "People see you walking and talking like a prince, dressing and eating like a prince. Let them think you're a prince. The important thing is that you know who you are."

The king overheard what Joseph said, and he was furious. He yelled, "My son still thinks he's a rooster! You said you'd make him better!"

"He is far better than he ever was before," said Joseph. "At first he was a show-off. Then he was silent and unhappy. Then he became a lunatic. But look at him now."

The king saw that his son was happy and relaxed, and that he was treating everyone very kindly.

"Who is better?" asked Joseph. "Someone who thinks he's a prince but shows off like a rooster? Or someone who thinks he's just a rooster but acts like a true prince?"

"You're right!" said the king. The prince got a great embrace, Joseph got a great reward and the king's gratitude, and the country got a great prince.

NOTE
Reb Nachman of Bratslav, Poland (1772–1810), is well known for this tale. He used this tale to explain how a wise teacher reaches out with understanding and earns a person's confidence. Only then can the teacher show the person by example how to improve and learn.

COMMENTARY
One could call this story a "how-to-educate-a-person" tale. Reb Nahman, no doubt, had in mind the relationship of a *rebbe* to his pupils, namely, how to turn them into Torah scholars. But before that could happen, he had to make *mentshn* (true human beings) of them by going to the level where he found them and bringing them to a higher level of learning. There is a great deal of time-tested wisdom in this "rooster" tale that we can apply to any learning situation—between parent and child, teacher and student, or therapist and patient. It is a story that can be understood on many levels. I call it the quintessential teaching story.

SOURCES AND VARIANTS

Maasiyiot U'Meshalim in *Kochavay Or*.

"The Turkey Prince" in *Rabbi Nachman's Stories*, translated by Rabbi Aryeh Kaplan.

This story appears in the "Nahman of Bratzlav" chapter in *Souls on Fire: Portraits and Legends of Hasidic Masters* by Elie Wiesel.

"The Prince Who Became a Rooster" in *101 Jewish Stories*, edited by Simon Certner.

"The Rooster Who Would Be King" in *Jewish Stories One Generation Tells Another*, retold by Peninnah Schram.

"The Prince Who Went Out of His Mind" in *Jewish Folktales*, retold by Pinhas Sadeh.

Tale Type: AT 1543C*—The clever doctor

Things Should Match

The Jewish people have tremendous respect for wise people. It's natural to think about how easy it is to be the opposite of a wise person: to be a fool. There are so many ways to act like a fool that the Jews have special colorful names for every type. We may feel foolish if someone tricks us, but sometimes we don't need anyone to make us look foolish—we can do it all by ourselves.

A *shlemiel* is the most common type of fool. No matter how bad things are, he always makes it worse. A shlemiel can't fall on his back without bruising his nose. A *shlimazel* is a fool who is also unlucky. A *nebeh* is a fool who is constantly blaming himself for being a fool.

For example, a shlemiel spills his soup, a shlimazel gets it spilled on himself, and a nebeh takes the blame and cleans up the mess.

There is also the *shmendrick*, the *shmo*, the *shlump,* and the *yold*. A shmendrick is a fool full of foolish hope. He may be weak and poor and hungry, but he keeps smiling, no matter what. A shmo doesn't know enough to smile, he doesn't have enough sense to know he's a fool. A shlump knows he is a fool, but he doesn't have the willpower to do anything about it. A yold is childishly foolish; he just has not learned anything yet.

For example, a shmendrick would be easily tricked into buying the Brooklyn Bridge. A shmo would lend the shmendrick the money to buy it. Why? Because the shmo couldn't think of a reason not to. A shlump would think of a hundred reasons not to, but he would lend the money anyway because he's too much of a shlump to say no. What about a yold? A yold would have no money to lend, but he would offer to help the shmendrick dismantle the bridge and carry it home.

There are so many tales about so many fools. This tale is about a shmendrick named Shmendrick.

SHMENDRICK, HIS WIFE, AND HIS TWELVE CHILDREN LIVED AT THE edge of the forest. They had a one-room cabin that they had built out of logs, with a roof of long thatched grass. They had a cow for milk, a sheep for wool, and some chickens for eggs. They also had a field and a garden, so they could grow whatever else they needed.

They always said to one another, "We don't have two coins to rub together, but except for that, we're quite well off."

One day, a man knocked on their door and said, "I'd like one of your chickens."

Shmendrick was very surprised. He answered, "I'll discuss it with my family." The family had a meeting to decide if they should give the man a chicken. An hour later, they came to a decision. They told the man, "We will let you have a chicken if you promise to take care of it."

"Certainly," said the man. "I am sure my whole family will love this chicken. What do you want for it?"

"We just want it to have a good home," said Shmendrick.

"I mean how much money do you want for it?" said the man.

"Oh!" said Shmendrick. "I didn't know you wanted to pay for it." The Shmendricks had never bought or sold anything before.

They had another meeting and decided how much money they wanted for the chicken. Shmendrick told the man, "Give us enough money so we can buy something."

The man smiled. He took the chicken, and he gave Shmendrick a small copper coin.

The Shmendricks sat around their old shaky table, staring at the coin. They had never bought anything before. They all tried to think of something they needed to buy. They couldn't think of anything.

Then Shmendrick said, "I lost a button from my shirt. Let's buy a button."

The Shmendrick family decided to buy the button together. They walked into town and stood outside the department store. They read out the words on the big sign over the door. The sign said, "We have everything that you need and even things that you don't." Shmendrick was very impressed. He told his wife and children, "This is the biggest and best store in the town." He was right because it was also the only store in town.

The Shmendricks were amazed at all the shelves full of things. Finally, they found the button department, and Shmendrick said to the salesclerk, "I want to buy a button."

The clerk loved to sell things, the more the better, so he said to

Shmendrick, "I can sell you a new button, but if you buy a new button, it won't match your old buttons. You need a set of six matching buttons."

Shmendrick said, "It's true. Things should match." So the salesman gave him a package of six matching buttons.

As Shmendrick turned to leave, the salesclerk in the next department pulled him over and said, "You shouldn't put fine new buttons on a ragged old shirt. It doesn't match. You need a new shirt."

Shmendrick said, "It's true. Things should match." That salesclerk brought him a new shirt and sewed on the new buttons right then and there.

The salesperson in the next department pulled Shmendrick aside. He said, "How can you wear that new shirt when the rest of your clothes are so old? You need a whole new outfit."

Shmendrick answered, "It's true. Things should match."

The salesclerk dressed him up in shiny shoes, silk socks, pants, jacket, tie, and a very sporty hat.

The salesperson in the next department saw how much Shmendrick was buying and called him over. He said, "How can you wear such fine new clothes when your wife and children are dressed in rags? They need new clothes as well."

Shmendrick looked at his wife and children and said, "It's true. Things should match."

So the wife and children got fine new clothes, but just as they were admiring each other, the salesclerk from the car department came over and said, "You are such a well-dressed family. You need a fine new car."

The whole Shmendrick family looked at one another and nodded. "It's true," they said. "Things should match."

The salesclerk showed them the best car on the lot. Everyone in the family was delighted. They bounced on the seats, pushed the buttons, honked the horn, and rolled the windows up and down as if it were the first time they'd ever been in a car. And, in fact, it was.

Another clerk dragged them out of the car and said, "You have fine new clothes and a fine new car. You need a fine new house!"

The Shmendricks thought about their shabby old cabin and said, "It's true. Things should match."

So the salesperson showed them a picture of the finest, newest house in town. "We'll take it!" said the Shmendricks.

Before they knew it, they were surrounded by salesclerks from every department, who showed them furniture, drapes, carpets, appliances, paintings for the walls, and so much more for their fine new house. Naturally, the Shmendricks agreed that they had to have it all. "After all," they said. "Things should match!"

Finally the day was ending. The department store was closing. The Shmendricks headed toward the door with so many boxes and packages and crates that everyone in the store had to help carry it all.

Just as they were leaving, the manager put his hand on Shmendrick's shoulder and whispered, "There's just one more thing."

"Another thing?" said Shmendrick. "We can't imagine one more thing that we could need."

"It's not what you need," said the manager with a polite smile. "It's what we need. How do you wish to pay for all of this?"

"Pay?" asked Shmendrick.

"Yes, pay," said the manager.

"We'll have to discuss it as a family," said Shmendrick. The family had a short meeting because they could see that the manager and salespeople were looking rather impatiently at them.

Finally Shmendrick said, "We can pay, but we may not be able to pay for all of it."

"How much money do you have?" asked the manager.

Shmendrick showed the manager the small copper coin.

"Oh," said the manager.

"Oh, oh," said the salespeople.

Oh, oh, oh! The manager and the salespeople started taking everything back. They took it back even faster than they had brought it out: the pets, sports equipment, toys, carpets, drapes, furniture, house, car, clothes, Shmendrick's shirt, all six brand-new buttons, except for one. The copper coin was just enough to pay for that one button.

The Shmendricks gathered their ragged clothes. They put them back on. They left the store and slowly and silently walked back to their worn-out old shack of a house. They sat around their shaky old table and stared at the button.

Mrs. Shmendrick said, "This button is the only thing we own that is brand new,"

The children nodded and said, "That's right. Everything else is old and worn out."

Shmendrick stood up and announced, "We're better off without it." He picked up the button and tossed it into the garbage. "After all," he said, "things should match."

COMMENTARY

These two main folk types, the shlemiel and the shlimazel, were developed in the European ghetto life, according to Nathan Ausubel. "True, they had their counterparts in the misfits and the maladjusted of all peoples, but who could compare with them in the extent and intensity of their almost comic wretchedness?" (343). For more about the schlemiels and schlimazels in Jewish folklore, see the various introductory notes throughout Nathan Ausubel's *A Treasury of Jewish Folklore*, the two categories in Leo Rosten's *The New Joys of Yiddish*, and Joseph Telushkin's *Jewish Humor*.

SOURCES AND VARIANTS

The closest variant I have found is "Ruined by a Pair of Shoelaces" in *The Wise Men of Chelm* by Samuel Tenenbaum. In this story, there is no button that starts the chain of events, but rather buying a new pair of shoelaces, then new shoes, and so on until they buy a new house, then new furniture. In the end, they have so many debts that they lose everything. "Mr. and Mrs. Dinkle had nothing new—not even new shoelaces. Since everything they now had was old and shabby, they were content" (28). This is a circular cumulative story, where the end parallels the beginning.

Another story comes to mind, "The Old Sandals" (IFA 8898) in *A Tale for Each Month 1970*, edited by Dov Noy, and collected by David Gid'on from his mother, Sarah, from Turkey. This is also a world folktale in which Abu Kasem, which means "father of fate" from Turkish and Arabic, gains a great deal of money. He buys a new house and new clothes, but he does not throw away his old comfortable worn-out sandals. Finally, when he buys shoes to match his new clothes, he has the problem of finding a way to get rid of his old sandals. This becomes the key motif of this story, rather than just focusing on getting everything to match. I have included my version of this story as the story-within-a-story in "We Never Lose Old Treasures" in *Stories Within Stories: From the Jewish Oral Tradition*, retold by Peninnah Schram.

Juha's Nail

By the 1900s much of the Jewish population who were living in Eastern and Western Europe or in North or South America were known as Ashkenazi Jews. Many of the Jews who had left Spain and Portugal after 1492 lived in the Arab world, ranging from North Africa across the Middle East all the way to India. They were called Sephardic Jews. Some of the Sephardim also went to Europe and North and South America. However, in many countries in the Middle East, including the Land of Israel, Yemen, Iraq, Iran, and Ethiopia, Jews were known by other names, such as Babylonian Jews (from Iran and Iraq) or Edot HaMizrakh (People of the East). However, Sephardic became an "umbrella" term, meaning all Jews other than Ashkenazi Jews. Because Jews are a pluralistic people, the customs, traditions, names, clothing, foods, and folklore (including their folktales) differed in many aspects. However, certain Jewish values, characters, and themes transcended any cultural differences.

This tale came from David Seruya, who was born in the early 1900s in a mountain village in Morocco, an Arab country in North Africa. His father spent his time in prayer and religious study, and he taught David his religious traditions and told him the spiritual stories of his people.

When David turned fifteen, two years after his Bar Mitzvah, he had to give up his studies and become a peddlar. He traveled by donkey to the city of Fez to buy merchandise. Then he would ride from village to village, selling spices, incense, needles and thread, mascara for makeup, bells for goats, and brass Hands of Fatima, which the Arabs nailed to their doors to protect their homes from evil. He might also have sold *mezuzahs* to his Jewish customers. A mezuzah is a small case that holds a parchment on which is written a sacred prayer with the name of God. Jews attach a mezuzah to each doorpost to protect their homes from evil.

David spent his childhood in a mountain village, listening to his father's religious tales. When he descended from the mountain to Fez, he heard very different stories, some of them quite shocking. This is a tale of foolishness told by the storytellers in the marketplace.

Juha was a well-known character in Arab tales. He could be surprisingly foolish, but he could also be surprisingly clever. The Jews of the Arab world often lived with uncertainty and insecurity, and so they appreciated surprises. They understood how life could suddenly change for the better or the worse—in the flash of a sword or in a flash of a clever idea.

In this next tale, even a fool like Juha can have a brilliant moment of cleverness, and a clever man like the camel merchant can have a dark moment of foolishness.

FOOLISH JUHA. CLEVER JUHA. JUHA SAT IN THE MARKETPLACE, smoking his small clay pipe, sipping his thick black coffee, listening and watching but never working. No one ever saw Juha working. Everyone told him, "Juha, you are a worthless fellow. Don't you know that you can't live without working?"

Juha answered, "When I need money I will just call out and ask for some."

The owner of the café said, "You fool, no one will give you money."

"I may be a fool," said Juha, "but I'm not the only fool, and I'm not the biggest fool."

One day it finally happened, Juha had no more money. Sure enough, he went into the market square, and he called out, "I need money. Will someone please give me money?"

Everyone laughed at Juha, especially the camel merchant, who always laughed the most at Juha. He said. "If I give you money, what will you give me? Do you have a camel that you can sell?"

"No, but I have a house," said Juha.

Juha had a good house with a fine courtyard.

The merchant said, "Give me your house, and I will give you ten thousand dinars."

"But my house is worth twenty thousand dinars," said Juha.

"A desperate man must take what he can get," said the merchant."

Juha answered, "I will sell you my house, but I will not sell you the big rusty nail above the front door. It stays mine, and it stays where it is."

"You've got a deal." The merchant laughed. "That nail is as worthless as you are. I got a bargain!"

They went to a lawyer and signed a contract. Juha got ten thousand dinars, and the merchant got Juha's house but not his nail. Juha still owned the nail above the door.

Juha moved out and sat in the marketplace, smoking his small clay pipe, sipping his thick black coffee, watching and listening but not working. Juha never worked.

A month went by, and Juha stood up, stretched himself, and

yawned. He said, "It's time to do some work."

"Work? Is Juha going to work?" everyone asked.

"Only a bit," said Juha. "Not too much."

Juha bought a very big cheese, a jar of yogurt, and a jug of milk. Then he bought some liver and kidneys, and an old fish that was beginning to smell. He stuffed it all into a big sack. He walked to his old house, and he hung the sack on the nail.

"Get that stinking thing away from my house!" the merchant yelled.

"The house belongs to you," said Juha, "but the nail belongs to me. That sack is hanging on my nail, so it stays where it is."

The merchant ran to the judge, but Juha showed the judge his contract. The merchant owned the house, but Juha owned the nail. He could hang his bag on his nail.

Then came the hot days, when the wind blew in from the desert. Everything in the sack began to rot. Horrible smells filled the house.

The man could not eat. He could not sleep. He could barely breathe. Juha kept sitting in the marketplace, puffing on his pipe and sipping his coffee. A week turned into a month, and a month turned into a nightmare. The sack stank worse and worse. The merchant's neighbors yelled at him, "That stinking thing is ruining the neighborhood!" They threw rotten food at him whenever he walked outside. Even his wife was furious. "We can't live here anymore!" she said. "We have to move!"

Finally the merchant went to Juha and said, "Take back your house."

"All right," said Juha. "I will buy the house for one thousand dinars."

"But I paid you ten thousand," said the merchant. "And you said it is worth twenty thousand!"

"It's not worth anything with that stinking sack over the door," said Juha.

"But I have to sell the house; I am desperate!" said the merchant.

Juha puffed on his pipe and sipped his coffee, and then he said, "Someone told me once that a desperate man must take what he can get."

The merchant shook his fists and yelled terrible things, but finally he sold the house to Juha for one thousand dinars. As the merchant turned to leave, Juha said loudly enough for everyone to hear, "I may be a fool, but I'm not the only fool, and I'm not the biggest fool."

So next time you think you're getting a bargain, remember Juha's nail. And the next time you call someone a fool, watch out. The fool may turn out to be you.

NOTE

Sephardic Jews: After the State of Israel was formed in 1948, almost all the Jews of the Arab nations emigrated there. Many of them left lands where Jews had been living for two thousand years. The two great Jewish cultures of Ashkenazi and Sephardic Jews are shaping the Israeli identity.

In the Middle Eastern countries, a storyteller in the marketplace made his living from the money that listeners gave him. To this day, if you go to the marketplace in Marrakesh, Morocco, you can still listen to the storytellers. The storyteller would often encourage his audience to be generous by ending his tale with an outstretched hand and the following words:

And the tale flows on just like the rivers,
And good listeners are good givers.

COMMENTARY

Tricksters are no doubt a part of every culture. These characters are often interchangeable in most of the trickster tales because they share many of the same qualities, namely, resourcefulness, trickery, clever reasoning, living-by-their-wits, survival instincts, and poverty, which is always accompanied by an enormous appetite. The trickster's sometimes outrageous where-nothing-is-sacred attitude allows the reader or listener to release tensions and fears as well as help gain a perspective of the social norms, identify what is forbidden in the society, and expose hypocrisy.

While usually wily and absurd in his actions and responses, the trickster is also naïve and innocent so that he sometimes dupes himself. Tamar Alexander, in the introduction to *Folktales of Joha: Jewish Trickster*, edited by Matilda Koen-Sarano, states it on the mark: "The naïve and childish Joha enables listeners to see things from the point of view of a game, to laugh at him from a position of superiority but at the same time to feel empathy and compassion" (14).

For example, one of the most popular trickster tales is the one in which the trickster arrives at the home of a wedding, figuring that he would get a free meal. But because he is dressed in torn, dirty clothes, he is not invited to the feast. However, when he returns wearing a handsome (borrowed) suit, he is then invited in with great honor. Seated at a table, the trickster stuffs the food into his pockets and pours the wine onto himself, too. He tells the stupefied guests that because the clothes have been invited to the feast, he is feeding them.

In world folklore, the Syrian fool, Djuha, appears in the Syrian variant "Djuha's Sleeve," the Turkish fool Nasr-ed-Din Hodja in "A Guest for Halil," the Greek fool in "The Hodja Feeds His Sleeves," and the Italian fool Giufa in a Sicilian version, "Eat Your Fill, My Fine Clothes." In addition, there are versions of this tale in the Israel Folktale Archives from Poland, Persia, Europe Ashkenazi, Yemen, and Afghanistan. My version, "Welcome to Clothes," is in *Tales of Elijah the Prophet*, retold by Peninnah Schram, with the character of Elijah the Prophet in the trickster role, and another version, "Going Along with Joha: A Medley of Mirth" in *Chosen Tales*, edited by Peninnah Schram.

One can easily tell from these titles that they are similar stories; they are widely popular among many Middle Eastern cultures as an important teaching tale regarding hospitality.

In the Jewish oral tradition, there are two popular trickster characters, Hershele Ostropolier, found in Eastern Europe Yiddish folktales, and Juha, the Arabic trickster, found in the Sephardic Middle Eastern folktales. The spellings for his name can vary: Juha, Joha, Djuha, Jha.

In addition to the Jewish and Arab tricksters, there are American trickster characters, such as Jack from Appalachia, and Coyote, Rabbit, Raven, and other animals as tricksters in the various Native American Indian folktales. For more about trickster tales, see *Trickster Tales: Forty Folk Stories from Around the World*, retold by Josepha Sherman.

Thus, you could hang almost any of the tricksters onto this type of tale. The lesson taught by the trickster, always in an outrageously humorous tale, would remain the same.

SOURCES AND VARIANTS
"Joha's Nail" in *Folktales of Joha: Jewish Trickster*, collected and edited by Matilda Koen-Sarano. Story narrated by M. Koen-Sarano, born in Milan, Italy, whose parents came from Turkey. She has been living in Israel since 1960.

IFA 16415, "Juha Sells His House," was told by David Seruya of Morocco, and recorded by Asher Ben Tzruya from Shlomi, Israel. It was published in Haya Bar-Itzhak and Aliza Shehar's *Jewish Moroccan Folk Narratives from Israel*.

A variant, "Jha's Nail," is found in Andre E. Elbaz's *Folktales of Canadian Sephardim*, collected from David Berdugo, who had heard it originally in French in Rabat. (In this version, Jha brings the carcass of a dead donkey to hang on the nail.)

IFA 9350 (Israel Arabic)—"The Nail of My Grandfather (Djoha)," recorded by Yfrah Haviv in 1972 as told by Salim Nadjyb (Arab Israeli) in Hebrew. This story has not been published.

Tale Type: AT 1542 *C (IFA)—**Man sells house, but for a nail.**
Motif: K 301—**Master thief**

What His Father Did

While the Arabic-transformed-Sephardic trickster Juha has appeared in an earlier story ("Juha's Nail"), we now have a story about the Eastern European trickster Hershel from Ostropol, known more familiarly as Hershele Ostropolier.

HERSHELE OSTROPOLIER WENT TO A INN AND BEGGED FOR A MEAL.

"No money, no meal," said the innkeeper.

Hershele pounded the table. He shouted, "If I don't get something to eat, I'm going to do what my father did." The innkeeper got scared and served Hershele a wonderful meal.

Hershele ate his fill, smiled peacefully and murmured, "Thank you."

Seeing that he was calmer after the meal, the curious innkeeper approached Hershele and asked, "Just tell me, when your father did not get something to eat, what did he do?"

"What could he do?" said Hershele, laughing. "He went hungry."

COMMENTARY

As with all tricksters, Hershele is a character in stories that have been attributed to other tricksters. As Nathan Ausubel writes, "They [trickster characters] have very often served conveniently as personality-pegs on which to hang a popular story or jest" (286).

Like some of the other pranksters, such as Nasr-ed-Din Hodja (Turkey) and Til Eulenspiegel (Germany), Hershele actually was a real person who helped to create folklore about himself. Born in the Ukraine (1757–1811), he earned his living by his wits and his words. In the years 1770–1810, he served as court "jester" for the Hasidic Rabbi Boruch of Miedziboz. Apparently this rabbi suffered from melancholia, so it was up to Hershele to lift his spirits with humorous stories and jests.

For more about tricksters, see the Commentary for "Joha's Nail," introductory notes in Nathan Ausubel's *A Treasury of Jewish Folklore*, Matilda Koen-Sarano's *Folktales of Joha: Jewish Trickster*, and Beatrice Silverman Weinreich's *Yiddish Folktales*.

SOURCES AND VARIANTS

"What Hershele's Father Did" in *A Treasury of Jewish Folklore*, edited by Nathan Ausubel.

Tales of Chelm

What if there were a place where everyone was a fool? A whole town of fools? The Town of Chelm was such a place.

There was no one to tell them how foolish they were, so the Chelmites considered themselves very wise. Chelm was full of serious, deep-thinking, respectable fools. They had their own mayor and town council, and every decision was thought out and voted for. And it was all nonsense. Here are four stories about the fools/wise men of Chelm.

The Wrong Kind of Horse

MERCHANTS WERE ALWAYS COMING TO CHELM TO SELL THINGS. They thought it would be easy to sell to a town full of fools, but it was not. An animal dealer tried to sell a tired old horse in the market. Everyone listened as he praised the horse for its strength and speed. He said, "This horse is so fast that you could leave Chelm at midnight and you'd be in Warsaw by four in the morning!" Suddenly everyone turned away. "What's wrong?" he asked.

"We don't want that horse," they said.

"Why not?" he asked.

"What are we going to do in Warsaw at four in the morning?"

How Not to Train a Cow

THE MERCHANT NEVER SOLD THAT HORSE, BUT HE DID SELL A COW to Chaim, the milkman. All went well till one day Chaim came into town without any milk to sell.

"What happened?" the people asked.

"Bad luck struck!" said Chaim. "I was about to make me a fortune from that cow."

"How?" they asked.

"I was training the cow to give milk without having to eat," he said. "That way I would have no expenses, just pure profit!"

"What went wrong?" they asked.

"Every day I trained the cow to eat a little less, then a little less," said Chaim. "Just when I got it to stop eating altogether, bad luck struck, and the cow died!"

A Lot of Sense

CHELM HAD PLENTY OF PEOPLE WITH HIGH HOPES FOR BUSINESS, like Sholem the fish merchant.

Sholem decided to go into business selling fish. He rented a store, filled it with fish, and hung out a sign that said FRESH FISH SOLD HERE DAILY.

"Why *fresh*?" asked his neighbor. "It's obvious that your fish are fresh. No one would think that you sell old fish."

"That makes sense," said Sholem, and he crossed out the word *fresh* so it read FISH SOLD HERE DAILY.

"Why *daily*?" asked another neighbor. "No one would think you sell only once a week. And why here? Of course they're sold here. This is your store. Where else would you sell them?"

"That also makes sense," said Sholem, so he crossed out *daily* and *here*. The sign read FISH SOLD.

"Why *sold*?" asked his friend. "What else would you do with your fish? Of course, you are selling them. They're not your pets."

"That makes sense, too," said Sholem, and he crossed out the word *sold* so the sign read FISH.

Just as he did, his other friends stopped by and asked, "Why *fish*? We know they aren't chickens or sheep. We can smell them a block away."

"It all makes so much sense," said Sholem. He crossed out the word *fish,* and he sat alone in his store with a blank sign over his window. He didn't get any customers for quite a while, but he kept telling himself, "That blank sign may not be good for business, but it makes a lot of sense."

Chelm Law

THE MAYOR OF CHELM VISITED SHOLEM TO SEE HOW HIS FISH store was doing. Sholom complained that business was bad, so the mayor bought his biggest fish, fresh and alive right out of the tank. Unfortunately, Sholem didn't have a bag, so the mayor had to carry the fish in his hands. The fish struggled to get free, and the mayor was embarrassed to be seen wrestling with a fish in public. He stuck the fish inside his shirt, buttoned up his jacket, and crossed his arms around it so the fish could not move.

"Now I've got him," said the mayor. But while the fish kept wriggling, the mayor held on, trying to look wise and respectable. He was almost home when he passed the town policeman, who saluted him. The mayor raised his arm and saluted back. That's all it took. The fish's tail poked out of the jacket and slapped the mayor hard across the face. What could the policeman do? He arrested the fish for assault and the attempted assassination of the mayor of Chelm.

The trial took a week. The fish was imprisoned in a fish tank in the courtroom. It was defended by Shlomo the fish merchant, who kept saying, "What else can you expect from a fish? It all makes so much sense." The jury discussed, debated, and voted. The fish was guilty. The penalty was death.

The next day at dawn, the policeman carried the fish out of the town, accompanied by the judge, the jury, the lawyers, and the mayor. They stood at the bridge and watched with serious faces as the policeman threw the fish into the river. The judge had sentenced the fish to death by drowning.

NOTE

In Yiddish, the Jewish vernacular language of the Eastern European Jews, there are even more colorful Jewish names for fools, such as s*hnook, shmegegge, ferd, lemech, nebech, naar, cham*, and the lowest fool, a *goilem*, which refers to a mindless monster made out clay brought magically to life.

Chelm is an actual city in southeast Poland and the oldest Jewish community, dating back to the eleventh century.

COMMENTARY

In Aarne and Thompson's *The Types of the Folktale*, the tale types for "Numskull Stories" number from 1,200 to 1,349. The "Fool of the World" stories are part of the folklore in many cultures. The original seems to have been the "Wise Men" of Schildburg (Germany). Chelm stories are identified as the Jewish "Fool of the World" stories. I recall reading, but cannot document, that it was in the late sixteenth century when the German stories were translated into Yiddish. Since folklore is fluid, the Jews of that area in Eastern Europe adapted the stories, transforming them into Jewish versions so that the stories reflected and expressed their Jewish identity, customs, religious traditions, names, and so on. How or why Chelm became the imaginary Jewish town of fools is not certain. There are several theories posited by folklorists, but Chelm it is. Even though Chelm is an actual place located in Poland, the folklore town bears no resemblance or connection to the geographical town, so they say. These humorous tales allow us to laugh and realize that we are all part Chelmite, sometimes.

It is the highest compliment to be called a Talmud *khakham* (a Torah scholar) among Jewishly educated people. However, the obverse of that expression of high regard would be to be called a *Khelemer nar* (a Chelm fool) or a *Khelemer khokhem* (a Chelm wise guy). Remember that wise man and fool are used synonymously and interchangeably in this type of story.

For more tales, see especially *The Wise Men of Helm and Their Merry Tales* and *More Wise Men of Helm and Their Merry Tales* by Solomon Simon; *The Wise Men of Chelm* by Samuel Tenenbaum; the sections "The Human Comedy" in *A Treasury of Jewish Folklore*, edited by Nathan Ausubel; and also "Nitwits, Wits, and Pranksters: Humorous Tales" in *Yiddish Folktales*, edited by Beatrice Silverman Weinreich.

"Chelm Law" is a universal story with variants in Finland, Sweden, England, France, Germany, Indonesia, Argentina, Africa, the Philippines, and many more places.

Tale Type: 1310—Drowning the crayfish as punishment
Motifs: K 581—Animal "punished" by being placed in favorite environment
J 1703—Town (country) of fools

A Holy Fool

The most special fools are holy fools. They are so foolish that they seem wise. Or perhaps they are so wise that they seem foolish. Decide for yourself. Schmelke of Nikolsburg was so completely unselfish that he did not think about being "sensible." The tale of Rabbi Schmelke of Nikolsburg is told more often as a story of religious virtue.

A BEGGAR CAME TO SHMELKE'S DOOR. THE BEGGAR ASKED SHMELKE for old or worn-out things, anything he did not need that the beggar might be able to use or sell.

"Just a moment," said Shmelke. He looked around his house and gave the beggar an old ring. Later, when Shmelke's wife found out what he had done, she was shocked. "What! There is a real diamond on that ring."

"I didn't know," said Schmelke. "It's too late now. I gave it away."

"Hurry. Maybe you can catch the beggar," she said.

Schmelke ran through the streets, searching everywhere till he saw the beggar standing on a corner trying to sell the ring to people passing by. "Stop!" said Shmelke. "Thank goodness I found you. That ring I gave you has a real diamond. It's worth a lot of money." Then he patted the beggar on the shoulder. "Be sure you get a fair price when you sell it."

COMMENTARY
Rabbi Shmelke of Nikolsburg (died 1778) was a disciple of Rabbi Dov Baer, the Maggid of Mezritch, known as the Great Maggid. Rabbi Shmelke loved to preach a sermon, but always with love rather than exhortation. He believed that words inspired by God are transforming. As Martin Buber writes in *Tales of the Hasidim: The Early Masters*, Rabbi Shmelke demanded two things from those who prayed: "First, that with the rivers of their love they wash away all separating walls and unite to one true congregation to furnish the site for the union with God; secondly, that they detach their prayers from individual wishes, and concentrate the full force of their being on the desire that God unite with his Shekhinah" (25–26). It seems that he really looked through a window and saw others rather than a mirror seeing only himself. (See the first part of "Which Way Should One Look—Up or Down?" in *Stories Within Stories: From the Jewish Oral Tradition*, retold by Peninnah Schram.) This story comes from eighteenth-century Eastern Europe.

SOURCES AND VARIANTS
"Rabbi Schmelke and the Beggar" (category "Charity") in *The Hasidic Anthology*, compiled by Louis I. Newman from J. Margoshes in the *Jewish Morning Journal* (Yiddish newspaper), November 18, 1932.

"The Ring" in *Tales of the Hasidim: The Early Masters* by Martin Buber.

"The Ring" in *Creating Angels: Stories of Tzedakah* by Barbara Diamond Goldin.

Which One Was More Blind?

Some people seem to be fools, but they turn out to be more clever than we are. It's a matter of perspective, after all.

A BLIND MAN WAS CARRYING A LANTERN AS HE WALKED DOWN A road in the dark. A driver saw him carrying the lantern and laughed. The driver stopped and said, "I've never seen anything so foolish. Why do you carry a light when you can't see anything with it?"

The blind man answered. "I am not carrying a light so I can see. I am carrying a light so drivers like you will see. I want you to see me so you won't run over me."

A Head Full of Dreams

Fools often daydream, spinning some fantastic scenarios, only to be brought abruptly back to earth. Listen to what happens to one such innocent fool.

YOSSEL WAS ALWAYS DREAMING THAT HE WAS RICH AND FAMOUS, but he was just a young fellow whose mother always had to call five times before he would even wake up. When he finally got out of bed, all he could do was talk about his dreams. He even sang about his dreams. He sang happily:

> I dreamed I was a millionaire.
> And everybody stopped to stare.
> I didn't have a single care
> Because I was a millionaire.

His mother said, "Were you dreaming about being a millionaire again?"

"Oh yes," said Yossel. "I'd give all the money in the world to be a millionaire!"

"But you don't have anything," said his mother, "except eggs. Here are ten eggs. Put them in a basket and carry them to the market. You can sell them for a penny apiece. That's ten cents."

Yossel headed to town, carrying the basket of eggs on his head. Before long Yossel was daydreaming. "If I had a hundred eggs, I'd get a hundred cents. But if I waited, the hundred eggs would hatch into a hundred chickens. Chickens are worth a dollar each, which means I'd get a hundred dollars. But if I waited, the hundred chickens would each lay a hundred eggs. I'd have a hundred hundred eggs! That's ten thousand eggs! But if I waited, those ten thousand eggs would hatch into ten thousand chickens. They'd be worth ten thousand dollars!"

Yossel walked slowly down the road, balancing the basket on his head as he thought about having ten thousand chickens worth ten thousand dollars.

"I wouldn't sell those ten thousand chickens. I'd wait till each chicken laid a hundred more eggs. That adds up to a million eggs! I'd wait for those million eggs to hatch. Then I'd have a million chickens that I could sell for a million dollars. And then I'd be a millionaire!"

Yossel grinned and strutted as he imagined being a millionaire. "I'd have fine clothes and a fine house, and everyone would say, 'Look! There's Yossel. He's so rich!' They would wave and clap, and I would say, 'Thank you, thank you,' and I would bow."

Then it happened. As Yossel bowed his head, the ten eggs he was carrying in the basket on his head rolled out and smashed onto the ground.

"What a mess!" Yosel moaned. "I was thinking so much about all the eggs that I didn't have, that now I've lost the ten eggs I really did have." As Yossel walked back home he sang sadly,

I dreamed I was a millionaire
And everybody stopped to stare
But nothing that I dreamed was there.
I'm just a millionaire of air!

COMMENTARY

The central motif of the broken eggs is a well-loved feature of many stories from all over the Mediterranean world. One favorite version is the Portuguese folktale called "An Expensive Omelette." However, in most versions, including in Louis Ginzberg's *The Legend of the Jews* and Micha Joseph Bin Gorion's *Mimekor Yisrael*, there is always a court case about a borrowed egg that was not returned and would have multiplied into a fortune. The case is argued usually before King

David. However, then it is the young Solomon who applies the more logical approach and brings the right perspective to the judgment (AT 920A, Part II—The suit over eggs). An egg for an egg.

I recall hearing a similar story about a poor man who receives a gift of a bottle of precious oil. He plans to eventually sell it, certain that it would bring him a fortune. Then the man begins to extrapolate what he will do with all that money: how he will marry and have a son, who will be so proud of him. But then, the thought occurs to him: what if the son disobeys him? Why then he would have to spank him. Acting out how he would do that, the man gestures wildly and knocks over the oil, which spills, spoiling his dreams (Motif: J2060.1—Foolish plans for the unborn child).

In my version, "The Boiled Eggs," in *Jewish Stories One Generation Tells Another*, retold by Peninnah Schram, I transposed the location of the story to an Eastern European *shtetl*, or small Jewish village. I also have a young woman resolve the case. Since she was as wise as my mother, I gave that character my mother's name.

Storytellers have always transformed stories from one century to another, from one locale to another, but this can be done only as long as it is credible to do so. So, too, with this version. The young man with a Yiddish name, Yossel, spins out his scenario of how wealthy he will become with his basket of eggs. But in the end, he has only yolk on his head. Daydreams can be fragile indeed.

SOURCES AND VARIANTS
Otsar Midrashim, Vol. I, collected and edited by Y. D. Eisenstein.

Variants of this tale appear in *The Exempla of the Rabbis* by Moses Gaster; in the section concerning Solomon in *Legends of the Jews*, VI, by Louis Ginzberg; as "The Borrowed Egg" In *Mimekor Yisrael*, edited by Micha Joseph Bin Gorion; as "The Egg" in *And It Came to Pass: Legends and Stories about King David and King Solomon*, told by Hayyim Nahman Bialik.

There is a version, "The Egg Seller Who Struck It Rich," in *Jewish Folktales* by Pinhas Sadeh from a book by Rabbi Yosef Hayyim of Baghdad, with an earlier version in the *Arabian Nights*.

"The Boiled Eggs" is in *Jewish Stories One Generation Tells Another*, retold by Peninnah Schram.

"The Case of the Hard-Boiled Eggs" is found in *Folktales of Joha: Jewish Trickster*, collected and edited by Matilda Koen-Sarano. It was narrated by Sara Yohay in 1991. (In this case, it is Joha who teaches the *kadi* (a Muslim judge) wisdom.)

Tale Type: AT 821B—Chickens from boiled eggs
Motifs: J 1191.2—Suit for chickens produced from boiled eggs
J 2061.1.2—Air-castle. Basket of eggs to be sold. In her excitement breaks all the eggs.

The Riddling Woman

This tale is clever, tricky, and wise. A clever riddle was used to trick a thoughtless person into acting wisely.

    The tale was told by the Jews of Yemen. Yemen claims to have been the home of the Queen of Sheba, and some say she was as wise as Solomon. The wise woman in this tale did not have Sheba's beauty, wealth, or power, but she did have some of her wisdom. She certainly knew how to deal with the young fellow in this story.

A FATHER WAS WORRIED ABOUT HIS SON. THE FATHER WORKED hard running a large business. The son did no work at all. He just wasted his time on foolish things. The father would ask his son to help him at work, but the son would ignore him or answer in a disrespectful way.

One day they had a loud argument. The son demanded more money. The father said he must earn his money by working. The son yelled, "I don't need to work. I am a rich man's son!" The father left the house with a troubled mind.

He was so upset that he walked beyond the town. Eventually he stopped at a stream for a drink of water. He noticed an old widowed woman with a cane. She was in a nearby field, planting seeds.

She smiled at him with her few teeth and said, "You look as tired as I feel. Sit down and rest. You can watch me work in my garden."

The father sat down and sighed. "Nevertheless?"

The old woman shook her head and said, "If I had, I would not have to."

The father was surprised. No one had ever understood what he meant when he said "Nevertheless?" This woman had understood and had given a clever answer.

The father asked, "Are the two still strong?"

She groaned and said, "There is a third one who helps."

"And what about the friends?" he asked.

This time she grinned and replied, "Their beds are too soft, so they became restless, and many have left."

"How are the brothers?" he asked.

The old woman looked closely at him. She answered, "They are getting closer."

The father laughed. He shook her hand. "You are a fine riddling woman," he told her. "Will you sell them?"

She nodded and replied, "Only to someone very hungry."

The father returned home in a good mood, but as soon as he walked through the door, his son approached him with another demand. "I want to take over the business," said the son. "Then I'll have all the money I want."

The father told him, "You have never worked, and you know nothing about the business. How can you do a proper job?"

"I have a good education, and I am smarter than you," said the son.

The father narrowed his eyes. He said, "If you know so much, then explain five riddles."

"Why should I?" asked the son.

"If you explain them, I will give you the business. If you don't, I will sell the business and give you nothing. Decide now."

"I will explain the riddles," said the son. "Test me."

His father said, "Each riddle is made up of a question and an answer.

"The first riddle asks, 'Nevertheless?' and its answer is, 'If I had, I would not have to.'

"The second riddle asks, 'Are the two still strong?' and its answer is, 'There is a third one who helps.'

"The third riddle asks, 'What about the friends?' The answer is,

'Their beds got too soft, so they became restless, and many have left.'

"The fourth riddle asks, 'How are the brothers?' The answer is, 'They are getting closer.'

"The fifth riddle asks, 'Will you sell them?' The reply is, 'Yes, but only to someone very hungry.' "

"Those riddles are impossible," said the son. "It isn't fair."

His father said, "I will give you a month and a day."

The young man pestered his father for clues, but it did no good. He asked everyone, but no one could help. In desperation, he tried thinking for himself; but since he had very little practice, he found thinking rather painful. When the morning of the final day arrived, the young man left the house with a troubled mind.

He walked for hours, thinking about the riddles. Eventually, he came to a stream far from town, and he noticed the old widowed woman with a cane.

"You look as tired as I feel," she said. "Sit down and rest. You can watch me work in my garden."

The young man sat down, and he repeated the riddles to himself. "Nevertheless," he muttered.

The old woman replied, "If I had, I would not have to."

The young man jumped up in amazement. "How do you know that?"

"I know many riddles," she said, and she repeated them all word for word.

"Tell me what they mean," the young man begged.

"You seem hungry to learn," she told him. "How much will you pay?"

"Anything," said the young man. He rushed home but found that he had no money saved. He had spent it all. So he sold everything he owned except the clothes that he was wearing. He hurried back and gave it all to her, saying, "Here's more money than you have ever seen. You will never have to work again."

"I accept it," said the old woman, "but I want more than your money."

"What else do you want?" asked the son.

"You have to earn what you want to learn," she said. "You must work at my side for one year and a day."

The young man argued, he begged, he threatened; but she would not change her mind.

The young man hurried home again and found his father just as the sun was setting. He was so worried and embarrassed that he spoke in a respectful way. He said, "Father, I found an old woman who can explain the riddles, but I need more time. Please let me have a year and a day."

"Why should I?" the father asked.

The young man bowed his head in shame. "The old woman said I have to earn what I want to learn."

His father understood what the riddling woman meant. He told his son, "I will give you the time, but do not waste it."

The young man went to work alongside the old woman, following all her instructions. He learned to work long and hard without complaining or giving up. At the end of the year and a day, the young man told her, "I did everything you asked. I planted and harvested and cooked the food I ate. I made the clothing that I wore. I built the bed that I slept in and the cabin that I lived in. Now please explain the riddles."

The old woman said, "You have listened to everything I told you. Now listen one last time. Your father saw me working in my field, and he asked me, 'Nevertheless?' which meant 'You are old. Why, nevertheless, do you work so hard?' I answered, 'If I had, I would not have to,' which means 'If I had help, I would not have to work so hard.'

"He asked, 'Are the two still strong?' which meant 'Are your two legs still strong?' I answered, 'There is a third one who helps. The third one is my cane. It is like a third leg that helps me walk.'

"He then asked, 'What about the friends?' which means 'What about your teeth, which should stay together as true friends do?' I answered, 'Their beds got too soft, so they became restless, and many have left,' which means 'My gums got too weak, so my teeth became loose, and many fell out.'

"He asked, 'How are the brothers?' which meant 'How are your two eyes?' I answered, 'They are getting closer,' which meant 'My eyes can't see well anymore, so they must get closer to things to see them properly.'

"Your father asked me, 'Will you sell them?' which meant 'Will you explain these riddles if someone pays you?' I answered, 'Only to someone very hungry.' You were very hungry to learn the answers, so you paid me well with your money and with your work."

"It's true," said the young man. He thanked the old woman from the bottom of his heart, then headed home. He was almost out of sight when he heard her shout, "Think about what else you learned. It is more important than any riddle."

As the son walked down the road, he thought deeply about the woman's parting words. He found his father waiting at the front door of his house, and he explained all the riddles.

The father was overjoyed. He embraced his son and told him, "The riddling woman has taught you well."

"I learned more than riddles from her. I learned how to plant and harvest and cook the food I ate. I learned to make the clothing that I wore and to build the bed I slept in and the cabin that I lived in. But more than that, I learned how to work long and hard without complaining and without giving up."

"You have earned what you have learned," said the father. "Now you can take over the business."

"I am not ready," said the young man. "I need another year and a day."

"Why?" asked the father in surprise.

The young man put his hand upon his father's shoulder and said, "I want to work at your side for a year and a day. I want to learn what you can teach me."

The father was happy to agree. The son worked and learned and made his father proud.

NOTE
Retelling a tale is different from repeating it. Sometimes retelling a tale means using different words or changing where or when a story happens. It can also mean changing the characters or changing parts of the story. For example, in this tale, I changed the riddler from an old man cutting wood to an old woman farming. I did this because the young man seemed to need an older woman's earthy wisdom. I showed the son to be selfish and arrogant, someone who really needed to change. I also showed how he was changed. I added to the ending by having the son ask his father to be his next teacher. I felt it would show that the son had found some real wisdom: he knew not only what he had learned, but also what he still needed to learn. I made many changes but was careful not to change the essential story.

COMMENTARY
Riddles have fascinated, entertained, and challenged people in many cultures, especially Jews. Certainly Arabic folktales are filled with riddles and questions. There are many riddle-filled stories in the Solomon and Sheba legends. But more than for entertainment, throughout the ages riddles often contained cryptic messages so that when there was danger to the Jewish communities, Jews could communicate through coded riddles.

A dictionary defines a riddle as "a question or statement so framed as to exercise one's ingenuity in answering it or discovering its meaning." When we solve the riddle, we often gain a new perspective, make new connections, and also stretch the mind.

In this story, there is a generational teacher-student relationship between the young man and the old woman (or old man, as in all the variants). Judaism demands respect for the elderly, who have lived a long time and have thereby gained the matured wisdom of experience. In Leviticus 19:32, it says: "Thou shalt rise up before the hoary head, and honor the face of the old man." Rabbi Joseph H. Hertz, in his commentary on this verse, writes: "A famous rabbi would stand up even before an aged heathen peasant and say, 'What storms of fortune has this old man weathered in his lifetime?'" Of course, this would hold true for a woman as well.

This story was told in both Eastern European and in Yemenite oral traditions. In every culture, we need to continue to value the wisdom and experience of the elderly, and young people need to be open to that understanding wisdom.

SOURCES AND VARIANTS
"The Plucked Pigeon" in *Yiddishe Folksmaises*, edited by Judah L. Cahan.
    "The Plucked Pigeon" in *A Treasury of Jewish Folklore*, edited by Nathan Ausubel.
    "Plucking the Rooster" in *Tales from the Wise Men of Israel* by Judith Ish-Kishor.
    "A Tale about a King and an Old Woodcutter" in *The Chambers of Yemen* by N. B. Gamliele.
    "The Woodcutter's Riddles" in *Jewish Stories One Generation Tells Another*, retold by Peninnah Schram.

The Hiding Place

By the 1800s the Jewish people were on the move again. Many emigrated from Europe to North and South America. Some headed to the Eretz Yisrael (Land of Israel) to try to create a Jewish state.

In 1948 Israel became a nation, and more Jews arrived. Some were volunteers from the United States and Canada, while others were survivors of the Holocaust. Then came the Sephardic Jews of the Arab nations. Many arrived with nothing more than they could carry, but one of their most important possessions took no space and had no price—it was their treasure of stories.

This next tale (and the two that follow it) had been told by the Jews in many different lands, wherever they lived or traveled. Now they continued to tell them in their new Jewish land.

Throughout the centuries, many countries had not allowed Jews to own land and become farmers because they were considered outsiders. They were also barred from going to university, so they had to find other ways to make a living. Some became tailors, shoemakers, and jewelers. Others became merchants. All of these were portable occupations.

Many remained merchants in North America. Some set up stores, while others traveled from town to town, buying and selling what they could. It could be dangerous to travel all alone, especially with merchandise and money, because there was so little protection. Sometimes a merchant's best protection was his intelligence and cleverness, as we see in this story.

A JEWISH MERCHANT NAMED RUBEN WAS TRAVELING FROM TOWN to town, buying and selling goods. As he approached a town that had many thieves, he decided to hide his money before he came to the center of the town. He stopped in a nearby field and buried a bag of a hundred dollars.

"It will be safe there," he said, and he went into town to conduct his business. When he returned to the hiding place, the money was gone. Someone must have seen him burying it, then dug it up when he left. But who?

Ruben looked around and noticed a grove of trees. He thought, "Someone could have watched me from behind those trees when I hid my money." Then he noticed boot prints in the dirt. He followed the tracks to a nearby farmhouse. There he saw a farmer in heavy boots standing in the yard feeding his horses. A shovel was leaning against the fence with fresh dirt on its blade.

Ruben was sure the farmer had taken his money, but he had no real proof. How could he get it back? He thought, "A thief will do anything for money. The only way a thief would give back my money would be if he somehow thought he would get more money for his trouble." Reuben smiled to himself. He had an idea.

"Hello, my friend," he called out as he approached the farmer.

"What do you want?" asked the farmer, looking suspicious.

"Only your advice," said Ruben. "I'm just coming back from town. I made a lot of money there, three hundred dollars."

The farmer's eyes lit up. "That is a lot of money. You shouldn't travel all alone with so much money. Somebody might rob you."

"You're right," Ruben answered. "I should hide it. I can get it back when I return with my friends."

"That's a good idea," said the farmer, looking excited.

"I could hide it with some other money that I hid nearby."

"Yes, hide it there," said the farmer.

"But what if someone discovers my hiding place? Then I'll lose the one hundred dollars and the three hundred dollars."

"Just check your hiding place," said the farmer. "If your hundred dollars is still there, then it's a safe place to hide the rest."

"I'll do it right now," said Ruben, turning to leave.

"Not yet," said the farmer, looking nervous. "Stay awhile. Let me make you something to eat."

The farmer invited Ruben into his house and cooked a fine meal for him. But as Ruben began to eat, the farmer said, "I have an important chore. I'll be right back."

Ruben was not surprised to see the farmer rush off with something heavy in his pocket. He ate and drank slowly, giving the farmer enough time to run to the hiding place in the field and bury the stolen bag of money.

The farmer returned breathless but very excited. "Did you enjoy your meal?" he asked.

"Oh yes," said Ruben. "But now I have to leave. I'm going to check my hiding place. If it's still safe, I'll hide the rest of my money there."

The farmer smiled, "That's exactly what you should do."

Ruben returned to the hiding place. Just as he had guessed, the farmer had returned the bag of money. Reuben looked out of the corner of his eye and glimpsed the farmer spying on him from behind the trees. Ruben slipped his hundred dollars out of the bag and then pretended to fill the bag with more and more money. He buried it as deeply as he could and hurried down the road. Ruben kept laughing as he thought to himself, "I wish I could stay and see the look on that thief's face when he digs up my bag and finds it full of dirt."

COMMENTARY

In Judaism, there are many commandments and warnings against stealing from others. "You shall not steal, neither deal falsely, neither lie one to another" (Leviticus XIX:11). There are punishments for those who take from others for selfish and illegitimate gain.

This tale is a universal folktale also found in Boccaccio's *Decameron*. There are fourteen parallels in the Israel Folktale Archives, including variants from Tunisia, Libya, Yemen, and Iraq. It also appears in Yiddish versions in the folklore of Eastern Europe. In one version from Iraq, it is the Arab neighbor who steals from his Jewish neighbor.

See also "The Rich Man's Reward" in this collection for another tale about money, honesty, and greed.

SOURCES AND VARIANTS

Meshal ha-Kadmoni II, by Yitshak ben Sahula.

Talmud Midrash *Aseret ha-Diberot*.

"The Story of a Hypocrite" in Micha Joseph Bin Gorion's *Mimekor Yisrael*, Book III.

"The Thief Who Was Too Clever" in Nathan Ausubel's *A Treasury of Jewish Folklore*.

"The Untrustworthy Innkeeper" in *101 Jewish Stories*, edited by Simon Certner.

IFA 7662—"The Clever Beggar and His Lost Money" was told by Morris Eyni from Iraq in *Faithful Guardians*, edited by Dov Noy.

Tale Type: AT 1617— Unjust banker deceived into delivering deposits

Motif: K 1667—Unjust banker deceived into delivering deposits by making him expect even larger amounts

The Crowded House

THE BRONSTEINS AND THEIR EIGHT CHILDREN, AS WELL AS MR. Bronstein's father and Mrs. Bronstein's mother, all lived together in a small house.

"What should we do?" asked Bronstein. "We can't make our house bigger, and we can't make our family smaller." So the whole family went to Reb Cohen, because Reb Cohen always had an answer.

"Reb Cohen, we're feeling so crowded," said Bronstein. "Our house is so small and our family is so big, we're always in one another's way. We're twisting and turning all through the house. What should we do?"

Reb Cohen tapped the side of his head. He stroked his beard, and finally he said, "I can tell you what to do, but you must do it and you must not ask me why."

"We promise," said the Bronsteins. "No questions."

"Do you have many relatives who live out of town?" he asked.

"Yes, we do," said Bronstein.

"Invite them to visit," said Reb Cohen. "And to stay over in your house."

"But, Reb Cohen," said Bronstein. "How will that help?"

"Remember your promise," said Reb Cohen. "No questions."

So Bronstein wrote to his brothers and sisters, and Mrs. Bronstein wrote to her uncles and aunts. They invited them to visit and to stay over in their house.

A week later, the whole Bronstein family went to Reb Cohen, along with all the brothers and sisters, the uncles and the aunts. "Reb Cohen," said Mrs. Bronstein. "The house is more crowded than before. We're still twisting and turning, but now with all the extra people, we're shifting and shuffling all through the house! You said that you could help. Tell us what we should do!"

"Mrs. Bronstein," said Reb Cohen, "do you have dogs and chickens?"

"Sure," said Mrs. Bronstein. "We've got two big dogs in the front yard and a flock of chickens in the back."

Reb Cohen told her, "Bring them all inside and keep them in the house."

"But why, Reb Cohen?"

"Remember your promise," said Reb Cohen. "No questions."

The Bronsteins brought in their dogs and chickens, and one week later they all came to Reb Cohen: the Bronstein family, the brothers and the sisters, the uncles and the aunts, the two dogs, and all the chickens.

"Reb Cohen," the Bronsteins shouted. "The house is more crowded than before. We're still twisting and turning, and we're shifting and shuffling; but now with all the dogs and chickens, we're stepping up and stepping over all through the house! Reb Cohen, you said that you could help. Tell us what we should do! Reb Cohen, you have to tell us what to do!"

Reb Cohen tapped the side of his head. He stroked his beard, and finally he said, "It's time to tell your guests to leave and to put out the dogs and chickens."

This time the Bronsteins didn't ask any questions. They said to their relatives, "Thank you for coming, but now you have to leave!" They put the dogs in the front yard. They put the chickens in the back, and they went inside and locked the door.

A week later the Bronsteins came to Reb Cohen. This time they were singing, "Oh, Reb Cohen, you're so smart, so wise, so clever! Now that everyone is gone, our house isn't crowded anymore. It feels so roomy!"

Reb Cohen asked, "You're not stepping up and stepping over? You're not shifting and shuffling? You're not twisting and turning?"

Bronstein laughed. "Reb Cohen, we're dancing! We're all dancing through our big roomy house!"

And the Bronsteins never felt crowded again.

COMMENTARY

This is probably one of the most popular tales, and it has been published in many versions as children's illustrated books. Sometimes people mistake this for a Sholem Aleichem story, but in fact it is a folktale, possibly originating as a Yiddish anecdote. Recently I was asked to be on the NPR radio program "The Infinite Mind," where they asked me to tell a version of this story as a way of illustrating the program's theme, "Satisfaction." As Ben Zoma says in Pirke Avot IV:1, "Who is rich? The man who is content with what he has."

This story is in the section "The Ancient Art of Reasoning" in *A Treasury of Jewish Folklore*. Ausubel writes: "The use of the Talmudic art of reasoning, tortuous and oblique in its technique as it may sometimes appear, is frequently applied in humorous tales. . . . Sometimes Talmudic logic by its realistic application finds common-sense answers to the most perplexing of human problems" (68).

Everything is relative. However, as we learn in many folktales, especially this one, it's all in the context and perspective.

SOURCES AND VARIANTS

In *A Treasury of Jewish Anecdotes* by Rabbi David Talner (1808–1882).

"It Could Always Be Worse" in *A Treasury of Jewish Folklore* by Nathan Ausubel.

"An Overcrowded House" in *My Grandmother's Stories* by Adele Geras.

"The Overcrowded House" in *Stories from Our Living Past* by Francine Prose.

Never Afraid Again

Sometimes people are tricked into doing something wrong. Sometimes they are tricked into doing something right.
    Here's a tale of a trick that was all for the best.

A GIRL NAMED HANNAH WAS AFRAID OF AN OLDER, BIGGER GIRL. She didn't want to tell anyone, but the longer she kept quiet, the more afraid she became. One day she heard two women talking outside a store in her neighborhood. One said, "I worked for someone who was very mean to me, but I went to an old woman named Yelda and asked for her help. She fixed everything just like magic."

Hannah thought, "Maybe Yelda can use magic to help me." She found out where the old woman lived and begged her to help.

Yelda asked, "Does the girl hurt you or steal from you or threaten you?"

"No, but she acts very mean," said Hannah. "Whenever I see her I feel frightened."

"I can help you," said Yelda. "Bring me three hairs of the scariest dog in the neighborhood."

"Will you use the hairs to make a magic spell?" Hannah asked. Yelda answered, "Never mind what I will do. Think about what you must do. Get me those three hairs, and you will have nothing to fear."

Hannah went to a huge guard dog that was chained behind a high fence. As she came close, the dog growled and pulled at its chain. She found one hair on the ground just outside the fence. The dog barked and lunged from the end of his chain, and Hannah ran for her life.

The next day Hannah returned. This time she waited by the fence until the dog became used to her. He stopped barking, and after a while he settled himself to sleep. She waited till he was asleep, then she reached into the yard and picked up another hair. The dog woke up. It barked and lunged, and Hannah ran for her life.

The third day was the most difficult. There were no more hairs on the ground. Hannah threw the dog a treat. He gobbled it but watched her suspiciously. She came back the next day with another treat. She visited the dog day after day, always giving him a treat. After a week, the dog was waiting for her and wagging his tail. Hannah carefully offered him a treat, and the dog ate it from her hand. The dog allowed her to pet him, and finally she was able to pull out a hair from his head.

She ran back to Old Yelda calling out, "Here are three hairs from the scariest dog in town. Use them in your magic. Put a spell on that mean girl so that I'll never be afraid of her again."

The old woman smiled and said, "I don't make magic spells."

"Then what will you do with the hairs?" she asked.

"Nothing at all," said Yelda. "You have already done everything all by yourself."

"What do you mean?" asked Hannah. "That bigger, older girl is just as mean as ever. She has not changed."

"You are the one who has changed," said Yelda. "You have trained yourself to be brave. Why be afraid of her when you have tamed the scariest dog in town?"

Suddenly Hannah realized how brave she really was, and she was no longer afraid.

NOTE

While Jews have lived in most parts of the world throughout the centuries, Jews came to America in its earliest years, escaping persecution and seeking freedom. Journeying has been an integral part of the Jewish experience. As always, the Jews carried with them their precious Torah and an appreciation for learning and storytelling.

The first Jew in America was also the first European in America. Luis de Torres sailed with Columbus in 1492, the day after the Jews were expelled from Spain. Torres was an expert in languages, so Columbus sent him ashore first to speak to the natives. Torres eventually started a plantation in Cuba and never returned to the Old World.

In 1654, twenty-three Jews, fleeing the Portuguese Inquisition in Recife, Brazil, reached the Dutch colony of New Amsterdam, which later became New York. They established the first Jewish community in the new country. Some had originally come from Germany, Poland, and Hungary; some from Turkey and Italy, and others mostly from Holland. These Ashkenzim and Sephardim were the "first settlers." They asked to buy a plot of land for a cemetery. They then organized a synagogue and a benevolent society so that they would not become a burden to the Dutch government. In 1755, Shearith Israel opened one of the earliest schools, combining secular and Hebrew education for the children. New York City now has the largest urban population of Jews in the world.

There were five waves of Jewish immigration to America. By the American Revolution (1776), there were between two thousand to three thousand Jews out of about three million people in the colonies. This was the first wave. The second wave was between 1830 and 1880, when approximately a quarter million Jews arrived in America, primarily from Central Europe. Then the third stream of Jewish immigrants—the huddled masses of about two million Jews—came in the last part of the 1800s. This was the mass migration from Eastern Europe escaping discriminations and persecutions. People kept coming from Eastern Europe up to World War I.

After World War II, refugees and survivors of Hitler's Holocaust made their way to the shores of America. This was the fourth wave of Jews coming to America. In more recent years, there has been a fifth wave of Jewish immigrants—from the former Soviet Union.

These three tales, "The Hiding Place," "The Crowded House," and "Never Afraid Again," have been told wherever Jews lived, but had been brought to "the golden land" and retold in America, too.

COMMENTARY

This is a universal tale with variants in Korean and African folktales. However, in all of these versions, it is the wife who wishes to find a love potion in order to win the heart of her warrior husband once again. In these tales, the woman must obtain either a tiger or a lion's whisker. However, the ending is the same, since courage or patience is already a trait the woman possesses in order to achieve her desired goal.

In this version of the story, the reteller changed the main character to a young girl who needs to find the courage and patience to deal with a school bully. She succeeds with a thoughtful plan.

The part where she brings the dog a treat each day until he gets to trust her reminds me of the Talmudic story and of the wise action of a young man who sets out to get the milk of a lioness, a needed remedy for the ill king. In order not to be attacked and devoured by a new mother lion, the young man tosses freshly slaughtered goat meat to the lioness. Each day the lioness allows the young man to come closer until he is finally able to obtain the milk. (See "The Great Debate" in Peninnah Schram's *Jewish Stories One Generation Tells Another*.)

SOURCES AND VARIANTS

"The Love Medicine" told by Tagabu Simon and recorded by Amela Einat in *Jewish Folktales from Ethiopia*, by Tamar Alexander and Amela Einat.

IFA 21307—"The Woman and the Lion," as told by an Ethiopian Jew and recorded by Berta Liber in 1999.

"Three Hairs of a Lion" in a Moroccan version from Fez is in Barbara Rush's *The Book of Jewish Women's Tales*.

Motif: B 848.2.1*—Woman removes lion's whisker without harm to self. Does this by patiently gaining lion's confidence with food and attentions. The lion's whisker required by wise man in order to make her husband love her. He suggests wooing husband with the same patience used on lion.

The Best Merchandise

One of the best-known tales told by the Jews of every land is called "The Best-Known-Merchandise."

A JEW IS ON A SHIP FILLED WITH MERCHANTS. THEY SHOW OFF their merchandise and ask the Jew, "What do you have?" He taps his head and says, "Everything I own is in here." They laugh and call him a fool.

Then a storm hits. The ship sinks, and everyone must swim to shore with nothing but the clothes he is wearing. They reach a city, but the merchants have nothing to sell. They have to beg in the street. A few days later, they see the Jew, well dressed and well fed. He drops some money in their begging cups, and they say to him, "We had so much merchandise, but now we have nothing. You had nothing, but now you have so much. How can it be?"

He taps his head and says, "I told you that everything I own is in here. I have studied all my life, and I have knowledge. I am working as a teacher."

The merchants nod their heads, and all agree, "Knowledge is the best merchandise."

NOTE
The Jewish people knew what it meant to lose everything and to have nothing, not even a home or a homeland. They survived by holding on to what could not be lost, stolen, or destroyed—knowledge. Each time they moved, they brought their best merchandise—knowledge of their Torah, history, their beliefs, their skills, and their stories. These stories cannot be lost, stolen, or destroyed, not as long as we keep remembering them and sharing them from generation to generation.

As Nathan Ausubel writes in *A Treasury of Jewish Folklore* about the lesson in this midrashic parable: "Ever since the Talmudic era, this saying has been on the lips of Jewish folk, uttered with a certainty and an intensity that has had few parallels in general lore" (32).

COMMENTARY
Jews have always valued education, generally, and Torah learning, specifically. Even with their innocent approach to life, the Chelmites understood something key about Judaism. One of the most telling jokes is the one about two Chelmites, one of whom is a Hebrew teacher. The teacher says to his friend, "If I were Rothschild, I'd be richer than Rothschild." The other Chelmite is amazed

and asks how that could be. After all, Rothschild is the wealthiest man in the world. The teacher answers simply, "Because I would do some teaching on the side." (See "Richer than Rothschild" in Nathan Ausubel's *A Treasury of Jewish Folklore*. This joke also appears in probably every book of Jewish humor.)

SOURCES AND VARIANTS
Babylonian Talmud, Mishpatim, and Nedarim 62A.
Hibbur Ma'assiyot Tanhuma, Terumah 1:2 (*Hibbur Ma'assiyot ve'ha'Midrashot*).
"The Merchandise of a Sage" in Micha Joseph Bin Gorion's *Mimekor Yisrael* II.
"Torah, the Best Merchandise" is in *Ma'aseh Book* by Moses Gaster.
"The Most Valuable Merchandise" is in *A Treasury of Jewish Folklore* by Nathan Ausubel.
"The Best Merchandise" is in Molly Cone's *Stories of Jewish Symbols*.
"The Best Merchandise" is in *A Child's Book of Midrash* by Barbara Diamond Goldin.

Motif: J 231.2*—Two merchants robbed. One with no merchandise but with knowledge in head makes way to wealth easily in new city.

Epilogue

WHAT HAPPENED TO STORYTELLING? FOLKTALES, LIKE FOLK MUSIC, WERE created by the people and passed on from generation to generation, especially in families and communities. That began to change in the last couple of hundred years as books became easily available. With the increased technology, people began to switch from sharing their traditional tales to reading literary stories created by authors. Then came movies and television, which provided more and more stories. Books, movies, television, and computers can produce very impressive stories for millions of people at a time. Yet, there is still something special and irreplaceable about a traditional tale told in the traditional way. Folktales are being kept alive in storytelling societies as well as in some families, schools, and summer camps. These stories contain truths and wisdom for all time. Try telling one of these tales yourself. You can bring an ancient story to life by telling it the way your ancestors did for thousands of years, from one person to another, face to face and heart to heart.

Glossary
by Peninnah Schram

Unless otherwise noted, the following expressions are Hebrew. Nearly all of them are used by Ashkenazim and Sephardim.

Agada (**Agadot,** plural)—Those sections of Talmud and Midrash containing homiletic expositions of Bible, stories, legends, folklore, anecdotes, and maxims; *Agada* is found throughout the Talmud, intermingling with *Halakha* (law), and deals with the spirit, rather than the letter, of the law.

Ashkenazi (**Ashkenazim,** plural)—Jews who come from Central or Eastern European areas. Their rituals and customs differ from those of the Sephardim. Ashkenazim speak Yiddish as their vernacular Jewish language. However, all Jews use Hebrew for prayer, for the Torah, and for other sacred texts.

Challah—A special white bread, usually braided, for Sabbath and holiday meals.

Dreidel—A spinning top, specifically used for a Hanukkah game. The four Hebrew letters on the dreidel stand for "a great miracle happened there."

Eshet Chayil—Woman of valor. These are the first words of Proverbs 31:10–31, describing the virtuous wife. The verses are chanted in the home on Friday evening (*erev Shabbat*).

Groggers—A noisemaker used during the public reading of the Megillah (the Scroll of Esther). Whenever the villain Haman's name is read, the noise of the groggers drowns out the sound of his name.

Haggadah—A book recounting the Exodus from Egypt and freedom from bondage. A compilation of poems, songs, psalms, and stories, it is recited at Passover seders in the home.

Hanukkah—Dedication. An eight-day festival, beginning Kislev 25, which commemorates the Maccabean victory over the Greek rulers of Syria and the rededication of the Temple in Jerusalem.

Hanukkiah—Hanukkah lamp, or menorah.

Hassid (**Hassidim**, plural)—"A pious one." A follower of Hassidism.

Havdalah—Distinction. The ceremony that marks the end of the Sabbath and festivals, and separates the holy day from the weekday.

IFA—Israel Folktale Archives, founded in 1956 by folklorist Dov Noy, are located at the Haifa University. Folklorists and volunteers have collected approximately twenty-three thousand folktales from the various ethnic communities in Israel. These tales are then classified according to tale types, motifs, and variants.

Khakham (Hebrew); **Khokhem** (Yiddish)—Wise person. A *Talmud khakham* is one who is learned in Torah and Talmud. However, a *Khelemer khokhem* is more of a "wise guy" and is dull-witted.

Khokhma—Wisdom.

Maggid—Teller. A traveling rabbi who teaches Judaism through stories.

Matza—Unleavened bread eaten during Passover.

Megillah—Hebrew scroll. There are five scrolls (*megillot*) of biblical Hagiographa: Ruth, Song of Songs, Lamentations, Ecclesiastes, and Esther. The Megillah of Esther is read on Purim and relates the story of Esther and Mordechai, who saved the Jews of the Persian Empire. The

Megillah usually refers to the Book of Esther.

Mezuzah—Doorpost. A parchment scroll with selected Torah verses placed in a decorative container and affixed to the doorpost of a Jewish home and to the doorpost of most rooms in the home. It serves as a protection for the home and each room.

Midrash (**midrashim**, plural)—That which is sought out. This is a genre of rabbinic legends that interprets and expands a biblical text in a story form. It can also refer to an individual interpretive story. The term refers to both the method of interpretation as well as to the legends themselves.

Mishna—The code of basic Jewish law (*halakhah*) redacted and arranged into six orders and subdivided into tractates by Rabbi Yehuda Hanasi, c. 200 C.E. Contains the Oral Law transmitted for generations.

Mitzva (**mitzvot**, plural)—A good deed; a commandment or precept.

Motif—The smallest element of a tale that is a recurrent thematic element used in a specific order to determine a tale type. Most motifs are used cross-culturally.

Passover—The festival of freedom that takes place in the spring on Nisan 15 and lasts for eight days (seven days in Israel). It commemorates the Exodus from Egypt.

Purim—A holiday that commemorates the Jews' victory over the evil Persian prime minister Haman. The defeat of the enemy was accomplished through the wisdom of Esther and Mordechai. This is a holiday of joyous celebration when the Scroll of Esther is read, and people dress in costume, give charity, and exchange gifts of pastries (especially hamantaschen), candies, and fruit.

Seder—Order. The order of service, including dinner, at the home on the first two nights of Passover. The religious home service, when the Haggadah is read.

Sephardi (**Sephardim**, plural)—The Jews who came from Spain and Portugal after their expulsion in 1492 and 1496, respectively, and who went to live in the Middle East, Eastern and Western Europe, and America. Sometimes the term refers to all Jews who are not Ashkenazim, since Sephardic rituals, customs, and folklore, for the most part, are different. Instead of Yiddish, Sephardim speak Ladino, which is Judeo-Spanish. However, all Jews, wherever they live, use the sacred language of Hebrew for prayer, for the Torah, and other sacred texts.

Shalom—Peace. Also used as a greeting to say hello or good-bye.

Shofar—A ram's horn and one of the oldest Jewish symbols. The blasts of the shofar are heard in the synagogue on the High Holy Days of Rosh Hashanah (Jewish New Year) and Yom Kippur (Day of Repentance).

Sukka—Booth. This is the temporary dwelling that the Israelites used while crossing the wilderness after they left Egypt. Jews also built these temporary huts while harvesting their crops. A sukka is built as part of the Sukkot festival to commemorate the harvest and to celebrate nature.

Sukkot—Booths. The harvest festival that begins on Tishri 15 and is known also as the Festival of Tabernacles.

Tale Type—The sequence of motifs that identifies a specific tale regardless of whatever changes or variables had been added in various countries and tellings. Some of the tale types are the same as motifs.

Talmud—The commentaries on the Torah and the Oral Law that were transmitted through the generations. There are two Talmuds: the Jerusalem Talmud and the Babylonian Talmud. The Babylonian Talmud has had the greatest influence on Jewish thought, study, and practice. It is a storehouse of Jewish history and customs intertwining *agada* (lore) and *halakha* (law). The Talmud is the most sacred Jewish text after the Bible and is comprised of the Mishna and the Gemara.

Torah—The first five books of the Bible, called the Five Books of Moses. The Torah is read aloud in the synagogue on Mondays, Thursdays, Sabbaths, and festivals, as long as a quorum of ten is present. Torah can also mean the entire body of Jewish teaching and sacred literature.

Tzedakah—Justice, charity.

Variant—A tale similar in theme to other tales but with changes that developed to reflect the specific ethnicity, culture, and geography of the group who tells it. However, having the same motif and tale type will identify the same tale, just a different version of it.

Yiddish—The Jewish vernacular language spoken by Ashkenazic Jews over the past thousand years. Its origin is Medieval German, but it is written in Hebrew letters and has a large Hebrew component. Yiddish is an amalgamation of several languages, including Hebrew, German, Slavic languages, and French.

Bibliography

Alexander, Tamar, and Amela Einat. *Jewish Folktales from Ethiopia* [in Hebrew]. Tel Aviv: Yediot Aharonot, 1996.

Alexander, Tamar, and Dov Noy, editors. *The Treasure of Our Fathers: Judeo-Spanish Tales* [in Hebrew]. Jerusalem: Misgav Yerushalaim, 1989.

Ausubel, Nathan, editor. *A Treasury of Jewish Folklore*. New York: Crown Publishing Group, 1989.

Bar-Itzhak, Haya, and Aliza Shehar. *Jewish Moroccan Folk Narratives from Israel*. Detroit: Wayne State University Press, 1993.

Benfrey, Theodor. *Pantscantantra*. Leipzig, 1859.

Ben ha-Melekh ve-ha-Nazir. Mantova, Italy, 1557.

Ben Naftali and Jeptha Yozpa, compilers. *Maaseh Nissim* [in Yiddish]. Amsterdam, 1696.

ben Sahula, Yitshak. *Meshal ha-Kadmoni II*. Frankfurt a.o., 1780.

Ben-Yehezkel, M. *The Book of Tales* [in Hebrew]. 2nd edition. Tel Aviv, 1957.

Bialik, Hayyim Nahman. *And It Came to Pass: Legends and Stories About King David and King Solomon*. New York: Hebrew Publishing Company, 1938.

Bialik, Hayyim Nahman, and Yehoshua Hana Ravnitzky, editors. *The Book of Legends: Legends from the Talmud and Midrash (Sefer Ha-Aggadah)*. Translated by William G. Braude. New York: Schocken Books, 1992.

Bin Gorion, Micha Joseph. *Der Born Judas*. Leipzig, 1916–21.

Bin Gorion, Micha Joseph. *Mimekor Yisrael*. Bloomington and London: Indiana University Press, 1976.

Bleefeld, Rabbi Bradley R., and Robert L. Shook. *Saving the World Entire and 100 Other Beloved Parables from the Talmud*. New York: Plume/Penguin Publishing, 1998.

Bloch, Chaim. *Gemeinde der Chassidim* [in German]. Vienna, 1920.

Buber, Martin. *Tales of the Hasidim: Early Masters*. New York: Schocken Books, 1947.

Bushnaq, Inea, editor and translator. *Arab Folktales*. New York: Pantheon, 1986.

Cahan, Judah L., editor. *Yiddishe Folksmaises* [in Yiddish]. New York and Vilna: Yiddishe Folklor Biblyotek, 1931.

Certner, Simon, editor. *101 Jewish Stories for Schools, Clubs and Camps*. New York: Jewish Education Committee Press, 1961.

Cheichel, Edna. *A Tale for Each Month 1967* [in Hebrew]. Haifa: IFA Publication Society, 1968.

Cohen, Malka. *Mipi Haham* [in Hebrew]. Tel Aviv: Yeda Am, 1974.

Cone, Molly. *Stories of Jewish Symbols*. New York: Bloch Publishers, 1963.

Cone, Molly. *Who Knows Ten?* New York: Union of American Hebrew Congregations, 1965.

Derenbourgue, Josef, editor. *Kalilah ve-Dimnah* (Deux Versions hebraiques du livre Kalilah et Dimnah). Paris, 1881.

Eisenstein, Y. D., editor. *Otsar Midrashim*. Volumes I-II. New York, 1915.

Elbaz, Andre E. *Folktales of Canadian Sephardim*. Toronto, Montreal, Winnipeg, Vancouver: Fitzhenry & Whiteside, 1982.

Epstein, Morris, editor and translator. *Mishlei Sindebar*. Philadelphia: Jewish Publication Society, 1967.

Frankel, Ellen. *The Classic Tales: 4,000 Years of Jewish Lore*. Northvale, New Jersey: Jason Aronson, 1989.

Frankel, Ellen, editor. *The Jewish Spirit: A Celebration in Stories and Art*. New York: Stewart, Tabori & Chang, 1998.

Gamliele, Nissim Benyamin. *The Chambers of Yemen* [in Hebrew] Tel Aviv: Afikim, 1978.

Gaster, Moses. *The Exempla of the Rabbis* (The Sefer ha-Ma'assiyot). London, 1924. (Also New York: Ktav, 1968.)

Gaster, Moses. *The Maaseh Book of Jewish Tales and Legends*. 2 vols. Philadelphia: Jewish Publication Society, 1934.

Geras, Adele. *My Grandmother's Stories: A Collection of Jewish Folk Tales*. New York: Alfred A. Knopf, 1990, 2003.

Ginzberg, Louis. *The Legends of the Jews*. 7 vols. Philadelphia: Jewish Publication Society, 1909–1938.

Glueckel of Hamelin. *The Memoirs of Glueckel of Hamelin*. Translated by Marvin Lowenthal. New York: Schocken Books, first published 1896, 1977.

Goldin, Barbara Diamond. *The Child's Book of Midrash: 52 Jewish Stories from the Sages*. Northvale, New Jersey: Jason Aronson, 1990.

Goldin, Barbara Diamond. *Creating Angels: Stories of Tzedakah*. Northvale, New Jersey: Jason Aronson, 1996.

Hadas, Moses, translator. *Fables of a Jewish Aesop*. Boston: Nonpariel Books, 2001.

Haggadot Ketu'ot in *Ha-Goren* IX, edited by S. A. Horodezky. Berlin, 1922.

ha-Nakdan, Berechiah. *Mishle Shu'alim* (Fox Fables) [in Hebrew]. Edited by L. Goldschmidt. Berlin: Erich Reiss, 1921. (Also Jerusalem: A. M. Habermann, 1946.)

Harlow, Jules, editor. *Lessons from Our Living Past*. New York: Behrman House, 1972.

Hazan, Abraham. *Kochvey Or* [in Hebrew]. Jerusalem, 1961. (Based on Rabbi Nahman of Nemirov's book published in 1896.) Also spelled *Kochavay Or*.

Heinemann, Benno. *The Maggid of Dubno and his Parables*. New York: Feldheim Publishers, 1978.

Heschel, Abraham Joshua. *The Sabbath: Its Meaning for Modern Man*. New York: Farrar, Straus and Giroux, 1951.

Hibbur Ma'assiyot Tanhuma, Terumah 1:2 (Hibbur Ma'assiyot ve'ha'Midrashot). Verona, 1647.

ibn Yahiya, Gedaliyah. *Shalshelet ha-Kabbalah*. Zolkiew, 1801.

Isaacs, Abram S. *Stories from the Rabbis*. New York: Charles L. Webster & Company, 1893. (Bloch, 1911)

Ish-Kishor, Judith. *Tales from the Wise Men of Israel*. Philadelphia: Lippincott, 1962.

Jaffe, Nina, and Steve Zeitlin. *While Standing on One Foot*. New York: Henry Holt, 1993.

Jellinek, Adolph, editor. *Midrash Aseret ha-Dibrot in Bet ha-Midrash*, Jerusalem: Wahrman Books, 1967.

Kagan, Ziporah, editor. *A Tale for Each Month 1963* (in Hebrew). Haifa: IFA Publication Series, 1964.

Kaplan. Rabbi Aryeh, translator. *Rabbi Nachman's Stories*. Brooklyn, New York: Breslov Research Institute, 1983.

Kehal Hasidim Hehadash, published in Lemberg in the early 19th century.

Kimmel, Eric A. *Days of Awe*. New York: Viking, 1991.

Koen-Sarano, Matilda, collector and editor. *Folktales of Joha: Jewish Trickster*. Translated by David Herman. Philadelphia: Jewish Publication Society, 2003.

Kranz, Jacob ben Wolf. *Kitve ha-Maggid mi-Dubno*, edited by Eliezer Steinman. Tel Aviv: Knesset Publishing, 1951.

Kumove, Shirley, compiler. *Words Like Arrows: A Collection of Yiddish Folk Sayings*. New York: Schocken Books, 1985.

The Life of Rabbi Nachman of Bratslav published in Lemberg, early 19th century.

Maasiyot U'Meshalim in *Kochavay Or*. Jerusalem, 1896/1972. [See Abraham Hazan above.]

Maimonides (Moses ben Maimon). *Mishneh Torah. Sefer Mada. Hilchot Teshuvah*, translated into English by Jonathan J. Baker, *Code of Maimonides. Book of Knowledge. Laws of Repentance*. From Web site: http://www.panix.com/~jjbaker/MadaT.html, July 21, 2004.

Maisel, Grace Ragues, and Samantha Shubert. *A Year of Jewish Stories: 52 Tales for Children and Their Families*. New York: UAHC Press, 2004.

Newman, Louis I., translator, selector, compiler, and arranger in collaboration with Samuel Spitz. *The Hasidic Anthology: Tales and Teachings of the Hasidim*. Northvale, New Jersey: Jason Aronson, 1987. Originally published by Charles Scribner's Sons in 1934 and by Schocken Books in 1963.

Novak, William, and Moshe Waldoks, editors and annotators. *The Big Book of Jewish Humor*. New York: Harper and Row, 1981.

Noy, Dov, editor. *Am Oved: Jewish-Iraqi Folktales*. Tel Aviv, 1965.

Noy, Dov, editor. *Faithful Guardians* [in Hebrew]. Collected by Zvi Moshe Haimovits. Haifa: IFA Publication Society, 1976.

Noy, Dov. *Folktales of Israel*. Chicago: University of Chicago Press, 1963.

Noy, Dov, editor and annotator. *The Golden Feather* [in Hebrew]. Collected by Moshe Attias. Haifa: IFA Publication Society, 1976.

Noy, Dov. *Jefet Schwili Tells: 195 Yemenite folktales* (German title: *Jefet Schwili Erzaehlt: 195 Jemenitische Volkserzaehlungen*). Berlin: Walter de Gruyter & Co., No. 96.

Noy, Dov, editor. *Sipurey Ba'aley Hayim* (The Jewish Oral Animal Tale) [in Hebrew]. Haifa: IFA Publication Society, 1976.

Noy, Dov, editor. *A Tale for Each Month 1970* [in Hebrew]. Haifa: IFA Publication Society, 1971.

Olsvanger, Immanuel, collector. *Rosinkes mit Mandlen: aus der Volksliteratur der Ostjuden, Schwanke, Erzahlungen, Sprichworter, und Ratzel Basel*. Verlag der Schweizerichen Gesellschaft fur Volkskunde, 1931.

Pavlat, Leo. *Jewish Folktales*. New York: Greenwich House, 1986.

Prose. Francine. *Stories from Our Living Past*. Edited by Jules Harlow. New York: Behrman House, 1974.

Rappoport, Angelo S. *The Folklore of the Jews*. London: The Soncino Press, 1937.

Rosten, Leo. *The New Joys of Yiddish*. Revised by Lawrence Bush. New York: Crown Publishers, 2001.

Rush, Barbara. *The Book of Jewish Women's Tales*. Northvale, New Jersey: Jason Aronson, 1994.

Sabar, Yona, editor and translator. *The Folk Literature of the Kurdistani Jews: An Anthology*. Yale Judaica Series. New Haven, Connecticut: Yale University Press, 1982.

Sadeh, Pinhas. *Jewish Folktales*, translated from the Hebrew by Hillel Halkin. New York: Doubleday, 1989.

Schram, Peninnah, editor. *Chosen Tales: Stories Told by Jewish Storytellers*. Northvale, New Jersey: Jason Aronson, 1995.

Schram, Peninnah. "Jewish Models: Adapting Folktales for Telling Aloud" in *Who Says? Essays on Pivotal Issues in Contemporary Storytelling*. Edited by Carol L. Birch and Melissa A. Heckler. Little Rock, Arkansas: August House Publishers, 1996.

Schram, Peninnah. *Jewish Stories One Generation Tells Another*. Northvale, New Jersey: Jason Aronson, 1987.

Schram, Peninnah. *Stories Within Stories: From the Jewish Oral Tradition*. Northvale, New Jersey: Jason Aronson, 2000.

Schram, Peninnah. *Tales of Elijah the Prophet*. Northvale, New Jersey: Jason Aronson, 1991.

Schwarzbaum, Haim. *Studies in Jewish and World Folklore*. Berlin: Walter De Gruyter & Co., 1968.

Schwartz, Cherie Karo. *Circle Spinning: Jewish Turning and Returning Tales*. Denver, Colorado: Hamsa Publications, 2002.

Schwartz, Howard, editor. *Gates to the New City: A Treasury of Modern Jewish Tales*. Northvale, New Jersey: Jason Aronson, 1991.

Schwartz, Howard, and Barbara Rush. *A Coat for the Moon and Other Jewish Tales*. Philadelphia: Jewish Publication Society, 1999.

Sefer ha-Bhiha veha-Hiddud.

Shenhar, Aliza, editor. *A Tale for Each Month 1973*. (Hebrew). Haifa: IFA Publication Society, 1974.

Sherman, Josepha. *Trickster Tales: Forty Folk Stories from Around the World*. Little Rock, Arkansas: August House Publishers, 1996.

Shteinman, Eliezer, editor. *Kitve ha-Maggid mi-Dubno*, Vol. 2. Tel Aviv: Keneset, 1953.

Sihot Hayim (chapbook). Piotrkov, s.a.

Simon, Solomon. *The Wise Men of Helm and Their Merry Tales* and *More Wise Men of Helm and Their Merry Tales*. New York: Behrman House, 1945.

Spiegel, Sholom. *Hebrew Reborn*. New York: Macmillan, 1930.

Steinsaltz, Adin. *The Talmud: the Steinsaltz Edition* (Talmud Bavli). New York: Random House, 1989.

Spalding, Henry D. *Encyclopedia of Jewish Humor: From Biblical Times to the Modern Age*. New York: Jonathan David, 1969.

Talmud Midrash, *Aseret ha-Diberot.*

Talner, Rabbi David. *A Treasury of Jewish Anecdotes.*

Telushkin, Rabbi Joseph. *Jewish Humor: What the Best Jewish Jokes Say About the Jews*. New York: William Morrow and Company, 1992.

Telushkin, Rabbi Joseph. *Jewish Wisdom*. New York: Morrow, 1994.

Tendlau, Abraham. *Spruchworter und Redensarten deutsch-judischer Vorzeit* [in German]. Frankfurt am Main: 1860.

Tenenbaum, Samuel. *The Wise Men of Chelm*. New York: Collier Books, 1965.

Weinreich, Beatrice Silverman. *Yiddish Folktales*. Translated by Leonard Wolf. New York: Pantheon Books, 1988.

Wiesel, Elie. *Souls on Fire: Portraits and Legends of Hasidic Masters*. New York: Random House, 1972.

Wistynezki, Yehuda Hacohen, editor. *Sefer Hasidim MN* (Mekitse Nirdamim). Berlin, 1891.

Yolen, Jane, editor. *Favorite Folktales from Around the World*. New York: Pantheon Books, 1986. The story "Rich Man, Poor Man," was originally published in Roger D. Abraham's *African Folktales*. New York: Pantheon Books, 1983.

Zevin, Rabbi Shlomo Yosef. *A Treasury of Chassidic Tales on the Torah*, Vol. 1. Translated by Uri Kaploun. Jerusalem and New York: Mesorah Publications in conjunction with Hillel Press, 1980.